P9-DVU-538

FICTION PZ 3 .L56684 Ma

Lessing, Doris May

The making of the
representative for Planet

South Dakota State Library Commission
Pierre, South Dakota

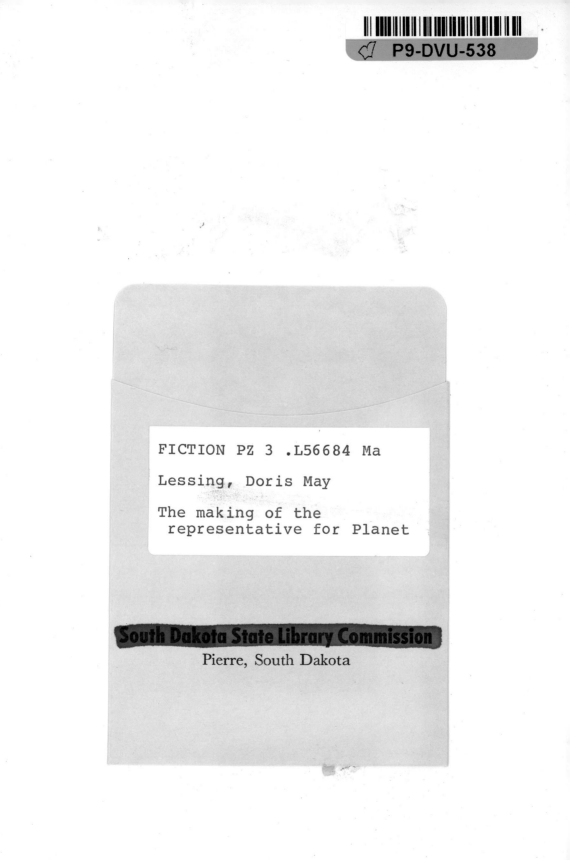

CANOPUS IN ARGOS: ARCHIVES

THE MAKING OF THE REPRESENTATIVE FOR PLANET 8

DORIS LESSING

FICTION
PZ
3
.L56684
ma

CANOPUS IN ARGOS: ARCHIVES

THE MAKING OF THE REPRESENTATIVE FOR PLANET 8

ALFRED A. KNOPF   NEW YORK   1982

This *is a* BORZOI BOOK
Published *by* ALFRED A. KNOPF, INC.

Copyright © 1982 *by Doris Lessing*
All rights reserved under International and Pan-American
Copyright Conventions.
Published in the United States by Alfred A. Knopf, Inc., New York.
Distributed by Random House, Inc., New York.
Grateful acknowledgment is made to John Murray
(Publishers), Ltd., for permission to reprint a portion
of Edward Wilson of the Antarctic by George Seaver.
Library of Congress Cataloging in Publication Data
Lessing, Doris May [date]
The Making of the representative for Planet 8.
(Canopus in argos: archives)
I. Title.
PR6023.E833M34   1982   823'.914   80-29073
ISBN 0-394-51906-X   AACR1
Manufactured in the United States of America
First Edition

This is the fourth in the novel-sequence
CANOPUS IN ARGOS: ARCHIVES.
The first was *Re: Colonised Planet 5, Shikasta.*
The second, *The Marriages Between Zones Three, Four, and Five.*
The third, *The Sirian Experiments.*
The fifth will be *The Sentimental Agents.*

CANOPUS IN ARGOS: ARCHIVES

THE MAKING OF THE REPRESENTATIVE FOR PLANET 8

You ask how the Canopean Agents seemed to us in the times of The Ice.

It was usually Johor who came, but whichever one of them it was, arrived without prior warning and apparently casually, stayed for a short or a long time, and during these agreeable visits—for we always looked forward to them—gave us advice, showed us how we could more effectively use the resources of our planet, suggested devices, methods, techniques. And then left without saying when we might expect to see Canopus again.

The Canopean Agents were not much unlike each other. I and the few others who had been taken to other Colonised Planets for instruction or training of various kinds knew that the officials of the Canopean Colonial Service were to be recognised by an authority they all had. But this was an expression of inner qualities, and not of a position in a hierarchy. On these other planets the Canopeans were always distinguishable from the natives, once we had learned what to look for. And this made us more aware of what it was they brought to our own Planet 8.

Everything on Planet 8 that had been planned, built, made— everything that was not natural—was according to their specifications. The presence of our kind on the planet was because of them: because of Canopus. They had brought us here, a species created by them from stock originating on several planets.

Therefore it is not accurate to talk of obedience: does one talk of *obeying* when it is a question of one's origin, and existence?

Or talk of rebellion . . .

There was once a near rebellion.

It was when Johor said we should circle our little globe with a tall thick wall, and brought instructions in how to make building substances not then known by us. We had to mix chemicals in certain proportions with our own crushed local stones. To make this wall would take all our strength, all our effort, and all our resources for a long time.

We pointed this out: as if it were likely Canopus did not already know it! This was our protest, for we called it that, among ourselves. And it was the limit of our "rebellion." Johor's smiling silence told us that a wall would have to be built.

What for?

We would find out, was the reply.

By the time the wall was completed, those who had been infants when it was started were old—I was one of them; and their children's children saw the ceremony when the last slab of shining black was swung into place on top of a construction fifty times as high as our tallest building, and with a breadth to match.

It was a marvel, this wall.

The black *thing* that circled our globe—though not at its widest part, not at its middle, a fact that made us question and doubt even more—drew us to it, attracted our minds and imaginations, absorbed us. Always were to be seen knots and groups and crowds of us, standing along its top; or on the observation platforms that had been placed all along it, for this purpose; or on high ground that overlooked it—high ground at a distance, for nothing near could give us an ample enough view. We were there in the early mornings when our sun flashed out over it, or at midday, when the glistening black flashed back light and colour to the sky, and at night, when the brilliant clustering stars of Planet 8 seemed to shine forth from within it as from dark water. Our planet did not have moons.

This wall had become our achievement, our progress, our summing up and definition: we were no longer developing in other ways, our wealth did not increase. We no longer expected, as we had in the past, always to be augmenting our resources: always to be making more subtle and fine and inventive our ways of living.

A wall. A great black shining wall. A *useless* wall.

Johor, the others who came, said: Wait, you will see, you will find out, you must trust us.

Their visits became more frequent, and their instructions were not always to do with the wall, and the nature and purposes of what we had to do were not easy to understand.

We knew that we had ceased to understand. We *had* understood—or believed we had—what Canopus wanted for us, and from us: we had been taking part, under their provision, in a long, slow progress upwards in civilisation.

During this period of change, while our expectations for ourselves and our children were being tempered, our world continued mild in climate, and agreeable, and very beautiful. As always, we continued to grow more crops and beasts than we needed, and exchanged these with other near planets for their surpluses. Our population remained at the exact level required of us by Canopus. Our wealth was not increasing but we were not poor. We had never suffered harshness or threat.

We were a favoured planet, climatically, physically. Other planets suffered extremes of climate, knew heat that flayed and withered, and cold that kept great parts of them uninhabitable. Planet 8's position from its sun was such that along a narrow central zone there was heat, and sometimes discomfort. Temperate zones spread on either side. At the poles were frigid regions: but these were very small. The planet did not incline on its axis, or only so little that it made no difference. We did not have seasons as we knew other planets did.

In the regions where we all lived, there was never snow or ice.

We would tell our children: "If you travel as far as you can that way, as far as you can that way, you will come to places that lie more distant from our sun than we do. You will find thick water, not light and quick-moving as it is with us. The water is slow with cold, and on its surface it wrinkles as it moves, or even, sometimes, makes plates or flakes that are solid. This is ice."

When, rarely, storms brought lumps of ice from the sky, a great thing was made of it; we called our children; we said: "Look, this is ice! At the poles of our world the cold slow water sometimes makes this substance, you might walk half a day and see no water that was not in this form: white, solid, glistening."

And, when they were older: "On some other planets as much of their surface is ice as on our planet is vegetation and fruitfulness."

We would say to them: "On our planet, in those regions lying back from the sun, sometimes from the sky fall small white flakes so light and so delicate you can blow them about and around with a breath. This is snow, this is how the water that is always in the air, though invisible to us, changes in those parts when it is frozen by the cold."

And the children would of course marvel and wonder and wish they might see snow, and the gelid wrinkling waters, and the ice that sometimes made crusts or even plates and sheets.

And then, snow fell.

Across light blue sunlit skies drove thick grey that came swarming down around us in a white fall, and everywhere we stood about, gazing up, gazing down, holding out our hands where the faint white flakes of the tales we told our children lay for an instant before they sank into blobs and smears of water.

It was not a prolonged fall, but it was heavy. One instant our world was as always, green and brown, and coloured with the shine and glisten of moving water, and the easy movement of light clouds. And the next it was a white world. Everywhere, white, and the black jut of the wall rising from it, and on the top of the black, a white crest.

Very often, looking back, we say that we did not understand clearly what was happening, the importance of an event. But I can say that this fall of white from our capacious and mild skies was something that struck into us, into our minds and our understandings. Oh yes, we knew, we understood. And, looking into each other's faces for confirmation of what we felt, it was there—the future.

That scene is as clear in my memory as any. We were all out of our dwellings, we had run together everywhere and were in groups and little crowds, and we were gazing into more than this cold white that had so suddenly enveloped us.

We were a tall lithe people, lightly but strongly built, and our colour was brown, and our eyes were black, and we had long straight black hair. We loved strong and vibrant colours in clothes and in the decoration of our houses: these were what we saw when we looked out at our world—the many blues of the sky, the infinite greens of the foliage, the reds and browns of our earth, mountains shining with pyrites and quartz, the dazzle of water and of sun.

We had not thought, ever, to wonder about our congruity with our surroundings, but on that day we did. We had never seemed to ourselves anything but comely, but against the white glisten that now covered everything we seemed to ourselves dingy and shrunken. Our skins were yellow, and our eyes puckered and strained because of the cold glare we could not escape except by shutting them. The strong colours of our clothes were harsh. We stood there shivering with the suddenness of the drop in temperature, and everywhere could be seen the same involuntary movement: of people looking at each other, finding what they saw ugly, and then, as they remembered that this was how they must be striking others, their eyes turning away, while they hugged themselves in their own arms not only because of the cold, but in a way that suggested a need for comfort, consolation.

Canopus arrived while the snow still lay, unmelted.

There were five of them, not the usual one, or two; and this alone was enough to impress us. They were among us while the snow melted so that our world returned to its warmth and the comfortable colours of growth—and while the snow again fell, and this time stayed for longer. Nor did they leave when this second affliction of white shrank and went. It was never the way of Canopus to demand, announce, threaten—or even to stand high on the crest of our wall, as we sometimes did on civic occasions, to address large crowds. No, they moved quietly among us, staying for a while in one dwelling, and then moving on to another, and while nothing dramatic or painful was ever said, before long we had all gathered from them what was needed.

The snow would come again, and more often; slowly the balance of warmth and cold on our planet would change, and there would be more snow and ice for us than there would be green and growth. And this and this and this was what we must do to prepare ourselves...

We were learning how those on harsher planets matched themselves against cold. We were hearing of houses built thick and strong to withstand weights of snow and the pressures of winds we had never known. We were told of clothing, and footwear, and how to wrap a head in thick cloth so that only the eyes would be exposed—this last impressed us fearfully, for the falls of snow we had seen had not done more than make us shiver and pull our light clothes more tightly around us.

While we were deciding how to make sure those settlements and towns nearest the poles would be protected first, we were told by Canopus that they should be abandoned altogether. All day and night, along that great black wall of ours, pressed crowds of people. We stood on it, we massed beside it. We laid our hands on the cold hard shine of it. We looked at the vast weight and thickness of it. We crowded close under it and looked up at how it towered and we felt it as a safety and guarantee. The wall—our wall—our great black useless monument, that had swallowed all our wealth and our labour and our thoughts and our capacities . . . it was going to save us all.

We were all now to live on one side of it, leaving the smaller part of our globe empty, for it would soon be uninhabitable. We travelled, many of us, all over those mild and agreeable lands where the crops were still in the fields, the vegetation many-coloured and warm. We were moving there, we knew, because of our need to comprehend. For we did not. One may be told something, act on it, trust in it—but that is not the same as *feeling* it, as a truth. We—those of us entrusted with the task of moving the populations out of their threatened homes—were always at work, in our imaginations, on the task of *really* knowing that shortly ice and snow would rule here. And those who had to submit to the move were not taking it in either.

Soon there were new towns and manufactories everywhere on the side of the wall that we believed would remain more or less as it had been . . . with perhaps snow and even storms, but not so very different from what we had known.

And now, when we stood gathered on the summit of that barrier wall that was going to have to hold the pressures of massing and thrusting ice, and gazed over a still fertile landscape where the future was not visible, except in the skies that had a pallid and pinched look, we felt grief, we were struck and slowed with grief, for at last we had become enabled to feel, really feel, in our substance, in our deepest selves, that our world, our way of living, everything we had been—was done, was over. Finished.

How dark it was, in our minds and our hopes, during that time of preparation, while we busied ourselves with resettling so many people in their new homes, while we took in what we could from Johor and the other emissaries they sent us.

And then we waited. Massing there—for we were now over-crowded and uncomfortable—on the inhabited part of our world, we came to think in this way: that at least the wall, that always visible reminder of our situation, was a proof that we had a future. Our planet had a future.

The time that passed then seemed long to us, and it was; but it was slowed, as well, by the events and thoughts that packed it. Our lives, from being easy, had become hard, the ideas that had inhabited our minds without being questioned were each one tested and—so far had everything changed for us—for the most part set aside.

The crops we had grown and that we were known for in all the near planets no longer thrived. The beasts we had understood and who understood us dwindled and went, and we had new strains of animal who, because their habits were to withstand hardship and threat, did not respond to us lovingly. We had not known how much of the happiness of our lives had been because, as we went among the fields and into the wilder places, we had always been greeted by affectionate creatures. I remember how I and some other representatives of cantons and provinces went out from a town we had used as a meeting place, into a valley we were accustomed to walk in for relaxation after our discussions; and where there had been a fresh bright green, and running streams, and light, quick, playful animals, there were hillsides covered with short, rough grey-ish plants and rocks growing new species of lichen, grey and thick, like fur—and there was a herd of heavy-shouldered, heavy-jawed cattle, all facing us, their horns lowered, great hooves planted solidly. And, as we stood, trying not to be dismayed, because we had learned to fear our grief, the greyish-brown of their shaggy hides lightened to silvery grey. The air was shedding greyish crumbs. We put out our hands and saw them fill with this rough grey substance. A grey sky seemed to lower itself, pulled down by the weight of itself. We stood there, shivering, pulling close the new clothes Canopus had told us to use, thick and warm and not easy to move about in, and we were there a long time, despite the cold, knowing that we needed such moments of sharp revelation so that we might change inwardly, to match our outward changes.

That part of our world beyond the wall was now grey and gelid and slow and cold, and filled with the creatures of the cold. First it was all bitter frosts, and flaking and then splitting stones, so that whole mountains changed their aspect, becoming littered and loose; and lowered and sullen skies, where clouds had become thick and dark—and then the snows came, showers and squalls of snow, and after that storms that raged a day, and then days at a time. Everything beyond our wall was white, and the new animals came crowding down towards us, their coats dragging with snow, their eyes looking sullenly out from the snow on their faces. But the snows melted, leaving the greys and the browns, and then came again—and again; and did not melt so quickly, and then did not melt at all.

Canopus said to us that we, the Representatives, should walk around our planet on the top of the wall. About fifty of us, then, set out; and Canopus came with us. The task took us almost a year. We walked into, not with, the revolving of the planet so that the sun always rose ahead of us, and we had to turn ourselves around when we wanted to see how the shadows gathered at nightfall. Because the top of the wall for the greater part of its way was so narrow, we walked no more than two or three abreast, and those at the back of this company had it brought into us how small and few we were under skies that on our right were packed with snow clouds. On the other side of the wall, but far down towards the pole, the skies were often still blue, and sometimes even warm, and down there were the greens and browns of a summery land, and the streams were quick and lively. To our right the grey and dour landscape was obscured again and again by snow. We could see that the whiteness of cold had claimed the far mountains on our right, and was covering the foothills and spreading out down the valleys.

And the winds that come pouring down from there hurt our lungs and made our eyes sting, so that we turned our heads away and looked down over the part of our world that still said to us, Welcome, here nature is as warm and as comfortable as your flesh. But Canopus kept directing us—gently, but making sure we did it—to look as much as we could into the world of cold.

And so we went, day after day, and it was as if we walked into a spreading blight, for soon, even on the left side of the wall we saw how grasses shrank and dimmed and vegetation lost its lustre, and the skies lowered themselves with a white glare somewhere behind the blue. And on the right the snows were reaching down, down, towards us, and our familiar landscapes were hard to recognise.

There was a day that we stood all together on our barrier wall, looking up into the freezing immensities, with Canopus among us, and we saw that the enormous heavy animals that Canopus had brought us from another of their planets were crowding close into the wall. They massed there, in vast herds, with the snow driving down behind them, and they were lifting their great heads and wild trapped eyes at the wall, which they could not cross. A short way ahead of us was a narrow gap which we had closed with a sliding door half the wall's height.

Canopus did not have to tell us what we must do. Some of us went down the side of the wall on to the rough soil, where the grasses had long since gone, leaving a thin crust of lichens, and pulled back the gates. The herds lifted their heads and swung their horns and trampled their feet in indecision, and then saw that this was their deliverance—and first one beast and then another charged through the gap, and soon from all over the frozen lands came charging and thundering herds of animals, and they all, one after another, went through the gap. What heavy clumsy beasts they were! We could never become accustomed to their mass and weight and ponderousness. On their heads were horns which at their base were thicker than our thighs, and sometimes they had four and even six horns. Their hooves left behind prints that would make small ponds. Their shoulders, to support these crests and clubs of bone, were like the slopes of hills. Their eyes were red and wild and suspicious, as if their fate was to query forever what had ordained them to carry such weights of bone and horn and meat and hair, for their coats hung down around them like tents.

These herds passed through the gap in our wall, taking twenty of our days to do it, and soon there were none of these beasts of the cold in that part of our world that was doomed to be swallowed by the cold. They were all in the more favoured parts—and we knew, without Canopus having to say anything to us, what it meant.

Had we really imagined that our guardian wall would contain all of the snow and ice and storm on one side of it, leaving everything on the other side warm and sweet? No, we had not; but we had not, either, really taken into our understandings that the threat would strike so hard into where we now all lived . . . into where we were crowding, massed, jostling together, with so much less of food and pleasantness that our former selves, our previous conditions, seemed like a dream of some distant and favoured planet that we only imagined we had known.

We stood there, looking into hills and valleys where grass still grew, though more thinly, and where the movement of water was still quick and free; we saw how the herds of the animals of the cold spread everywhere, making our ears ring and hurt with their savage exulting bellowing because they had found some grass. We were a company of thin yellow light-boned birdlike creatures, engulfed in the thick pelts of the herds, wildly gazing at a landscape that no longer matched us. And, as we had taken to doing more and more, we gazed up, our eyes kept returning to the skies, where the birds moved easily. No, they were not the small and pretty birds of the warm times, flocks and groups and assemblies darting and swirling and swooping as one, moving as fast as water does when its molecules are dancing. They were the birds of this chilly time, individual, eagles and hawks and buzzards, moving slowly on wings that did not beat, but balanced. They too had heavy shoulders and their eyes glared from thick feathers, and they circled and swept about the skies on the breath of freezing winds that had killed our familiar flocks sometimes as they flew; so that, seeing the little brightly coloured bodies drop from the air, we had looked up and imagined we could see, too, the freezing blast that had struck them down out of the sky. But they were birds, these great savage creatures; they could move; they could sweep from one end of a valley to the other in the time we could hold a breath. We had once been as they were, we told ourselves, as we stood there on the wall slowed and clumsy in our thick skins—the wall which, on the side towards the ice, was dimmed and clouded, no longer a brilliant shining black, but shades of grey. Frosted grey.

Now that the herds had all gone through the wall, we filled the gap by pushing across the gate. But Canopus said that as soon as we got back to our homes, work parties must be sent out, and this gap, and the others that had been left, must be built up as strongly and thickly as all the rest of the wall. For the openings that had been ordered to be left in the wall long before there had been cold, or even the first signs of cold, to save animals that had not even been brought to our planet, had fulfilled their purpose. We no longer needed them. The wall must be perfect and whole and without a weak place.

We walked on for some days after that before there was a blizzard of an intensity we had not even been able to imagine. We huddled on the safe side of the wall, while the winds screamed over us and sometimes came sucking and driving down where we were, and we shivered and we shrank, and knew that we had not begun to imagine what we had, all of us, to face. And when the screaming and scouring stopped and we climbed up the little projecting steps to the top, carefully because of the glaze of ice on them, we saw that on the cold side snow had fallen so heavily that all the hollows and the heights of the landscape were filled in with billowy white, and the wall was only half its previous height.

By then we were not far from our starting place, and we all longed to be back in our homes, our new thick-walled solid houses with roofs that had been pitched to throw off any snowfall—so we had thought. But now wondered. Were we going to have to live under snow as some creatures lived under water? Were we going to have to make little tunnels and caves for ourselves under a world of snow?

But still, on our side of the wall, where our towns and cities and farms spread, there was some green, there was the shine of moving water. And knowing of our hunger and our desperation and our longing, Canopus did not now make us turn our faces from this livingness, but allowed us to stumble on, looking warmthwards, trying to ignore the snowy wilderness that was crowding down on us.

And it was during these days that Johor fell back with me, and talked to me, alone. I listened to him and I had my eyes on my fellows in front, the Representatives, and when I knew that what I was being told was for me, and not for them—not yet, at least, because they could not yet face it—there came into me an even deeper sense of what was in store. But what worse could there possibly be?

Ahead of us this great wall of ours stood high and black above marshes where the snows of the blizzard had partly melted, leaving streaks and blobs of thin white on dark water. We stood there, Johor and I, and watched our companions walk away, and become no more than a moving blur on the crest of the wall where it rose to cross a ridge and then disappeared from our view. It climbed again, and we saw it, still mighty and tall though so far away, showing exactly what its nature was, for on one side the snows piled, and on the other the beasts fed on wintry grass and on low grey bushes.

Johor touched my arm, and we walked forward to stand where the marshes lay on either side. On the right the dark white-streaked waters seemed channels to the world of snow and ice. But on the other side the marshes were an estuary which led to the ocean. We called it that, though it was really a large lake, enclosed by land. We had been told of, and some of us had seen, planets that were more water than land—where lumps and pieces and even large areas of land were in watery immensities. It is hard to believe in something very far from experience. With us everything was the other way about. Our "ocean" was always a marvel to us. Was precious. Our lives depended on it, we knew that, for it helped us to make our atmosphere. It seemed to us to represent distant and rare truths, was a symbol to us of what was hard to attain and must be guarded and sheltered. Those of you who live on planets where liquids are as common as earth and rocks and sand will find it as hard to imagine our cherishing of this "ocean" of ours as we found it to visualise planets where water masses bathed the whole globe in a continuous living movement, speaking always of wholeness, oneness, interaction, of rapid and easy interchange. For the basis of our lives, the substance which bound us in continuity, was earth. Oh yes, we knew that this soil and rock that made our planet, with water held so shallowly in it, and only in one place, except for the streams and rivers that fed it, was something that moved, just as water moved—we knew rock had its currents, like water. We knew it because Canopus had taught us to think like this. Solidity, immobility, permanence—this was only how we with our Planet 8 eyes had to see things. Nowhere, said Canopus, was permanence, was immutability—not anywhere in the galaxy, or the universe. There was nothing that did not move and change. When we looked at a stone, we must think of it as a dance and a flow. And at a hillside. Or a mountain.

I was standing there with my back to the icy winds, face towards our precious lake that was out of sight beyond tall plumy reeds, and I was thinking: And ice?—we must see this new enemy of ours as something all fluidity and movement? And it was at that moment that it came into me for the first time that our ocean might freeze. Even though it was on the "safe" side of our barrier wall. The thought came like a blast of cold. I knew it would be so, and I already felt something of what Canopus was going to tell me. I did not want to turn and face Johor—face what I had to.

I felt his touch on my elbow again and I did turn.

I saw him as he saw me, fragile and vulnerable inside thick pelts, hands hidden inside sleeves, eyes peering out from deep shaggy hoods.

It is a hard thing, to lose the sense of physical appropriateness— and again my eyes went skywards where an eagle lay poised on air just above us.

"Representative," said Johor gently, and I made my gaze return downwards, to what I could see of his yellow face.

"Your ocean will freeze," he said.

I could feel my bones huddle and tremble inside my thin flesh.

I tried to joke: "Canopus can bring us new beasts with heavy bones for the cold—but what can you do for our bones? Or shall we all die out as our other animals did, to make way for new species—new races?"

"You will not die out," he said, and his strong brown eyes—inflamed though, and strained—were forcing me to look at him.

Another new thought came into me, and I asked: "You were not born on Canopus, so you said. What kind of planet did you come from?"

"I was given existence on a warm and easy planet."

"As Planet 8 was, once."

"As the planet is that you will all be going to."

At this I was silent for a very long time. There were too many adjustments to make in my thoughts—which whirled about and did not settle into patterns that could frame useful questions.

When I was slightly recovered, I still was facing Johor, who stood with his back to a wind that came pouring down from the snow fields.

"You are always travelling," I said. "You are seldom on your own planet—do you miss it?"

He did not answer. He was waiting.

"If we are all to be space-lifted away from our home, then why the wall? Why were we not taken away when the snows first began to fall?"

"The hardest thing for any one of us to realise—every one of us, no matter how high in the levels of functioning—is that we are all subject to an overall plan. A general Necessity."

"It was not convenient?" And my voice was bitter.

"When we took you for training to the other planets, did you ever hear of the planet Rohanda?"

I had, and my curiosity was already expectation—and even a warm and friendly expectation.

"Yes, it is a beautiful planet. And quite one of our most successful attempts. . . ." He smiled, though I could not see his smile, only the change in the shape of his eyes, for his mouth was covered: and I smiled too—ruefully, of course. For it is not easy to accept oneself as an item among many.

"Our poor planet is not a successful attempt!"

"It is not anyone's fault," he said. "The Alignments have changed . . . unexpectedly. We believed that Planet 8 was destined for stability and slow growth. As things have not turned out that way, we mean to take you to Rohanda. But first another phase of development there must be concluded. It is a question of raising a certain species there to a level where, when your kind are brought in, you will make a harmonious whole. That is not yet. Meanwhile you, on this planet, must be sheltered from the worst of what will happen."

"The wall, then, is something to hold off the worst of the snow?"

"The worst of the ice that will come pressing down in great sheets and plates and will rise against the wall. Down there, where we look now . . ." and he turned me about to face away from the cold towards the warm pole, "it will be bad enough. You may have a hard time of it, surviving. And this wall will hold, so we believe, the force of the ice. For long enough."

"And you do not want us all to know that we must leave our Home Planet for Rohanda?"

"It is enough that one of you knows."

It took time to digest this. Time and observation. For without my ever telling anyone at all, not even the other Representatives, it became known that we would all be space-lifted to another beautiful warm planet, where our lives would become again as they had once been—in a past that seemed so far from us. Though it was not far, only on the other side of the physical change in our lives that had been so sharp and sudden that we could hardly believe what we had been.

Johor and the other Canopeans left us, having made sure that all the gaps in our wall were well and strongly filled. And that no living thing was left on the cold side of the wall. It seemed a dead place, where now the blizzards raged almost continuously, the winds howled and shrieked, and the snows heaped themselves up and up so that even the mountains seemed likely to become buried. And then, standing on our wall to gaze there, our gloved hands held to shield our streaming eyes, we saw that the mountains had a glassy look, and that between the foothills crept tongues of ice. A few of us did wrap ourselves, and made little carts that could slide on runners, and we ventured up into that frigid and horrible land to find out what we could. It was like a journey into another part of ourselves, so slowed and difficult were our movements, so painful the breaths we had to take. All we could see was that the snows piled up, up, into the skies, and the packs of ice crept down. And, this expedition over, we stood huddled on our wall, looking at where we had been, and saw how the snow came smoking off fields of white and eddied up into skies that were a hard cold blue.

We had a great deal to do, all of us, and most particularly we Representatives. The physical problems, bad enough, were the least of it. Now that it had spread from mind to mind that we had a home waiting for us, in a favoured part of the galaxy, where we could again be congruous with our surroundings, a quick-moving, shining-brown-skinned, healthy race under blue skies—now that this dream had taken hold of us, our present realities seemed to numb us even more. And when we looked up and saw how the snows had massed themselves into packs of gleaming ice with great cracks that could run from one horizon to another—this present horror came to seem less real to us than Rohanda, where we were bound. When? We were coming to yearn, to long, for our deliverance, and against this I and the others had to fight. For if we allowed ourselves to lapse into daydreams and longings, then none of us would be alive to make that final journey to the lovely planet.

One of our difficulties was that when our peoples had been moved away from the cold, everything that had been built to shelter them and their beasts faced away from the blizzards. Standing on the wall, what had to strike us first was how villages and towns huddled and crept and hid away, and there seemed no windows or openings, for these were on the other side. Before, our towns had been spread about and seemed haphazard, as towns do, when built to catch the advantages of an amenable slope, or of a fertile wind. Now, as we looked down, a town might seem like a single building, in which one might walk from room to room through a valley. So vulnerable they looked, our new homes, so easily crushed, as we stood high there, feeling the winds tear and buffet us, knowing the strength of what was to come—and yet, down again at earth level, inside a town, it was easy to forget what threatened. It was sheltered, for the winds streamed above. All the apertures showed hills still green, and mountains green for a good part of the way up to their summits, and there was the glint and shine of water, and patches of misty blue appeared among the thick grey of the cloud. Down there was fertility and warmth and pleasantness . . . At the margins of the eye's reach was our heart's desire.

What were we to do, then, we Representatives? Force these people for whom we were responsible to look back—look up? There behind them was the rampart of the wall, so high from these low huddles they lived in that a third of the sky was blocked out. A wall like a cliff, a sheer black shining cliff. Still black on this side, though if you stood close to it and gazed into the shine that had once mirrored blue skies where the white clouds of what now seemed an interminable summer ambled and lazed, it could be seen that the smooth black had a faint grey bloom. Could be seen that the minutest scratchiest lines marred the shine. Frost. And in the early mornings the whole glossy surface had a crumbling grey look to it.

Were we to insist that every individual in the land climb up the steps to the top of the wall and look icewards, feel the threat of the gale, know what lay there always on the other side of the wall? We were to make a ritual of it, perhaps?

Often enough we, the fifty or so of us, would climb up there to look out and up to the cold pole for new changes and threats—and debate how to combat this weakening mood among the people.

Perhaps it was the extent of the changes that prevented us. A world of snow—was how we had thought of it. But it was ice now. The snow had packed, had massed, had gone hard and heavy. A ringing world—a stone flung on to it reverberated. It seemed to us as we stood high there, the wind in our faces, that a bird swooping past could make the ice sing and thrum. And when the blizzards came, the winds drove snow masses up into the air, whirled them around the hard clanging skies and dropped them again, to slide and swirl into new piles and drifts. Soon to freeze again and make new ice packs that came driving down the valleys towards us. Now as we looked out, we had to remind ourselves of the real height of the barrier wall by glancing down behind us to the sheltered side, for the snows were more than halfway up the wall. Quite soon—we joked—we would be able to step off the top of that wall and simply walk off on snow. Or on ice.

We decided not to institute rituals of snow-watching and wall-climbing, or make strong songs to combat the soft wailing yearning songs that now were heard all day and half the night. We did not really know how to assess the effects that such forced submersions in reality might have.

Once we had known exactly what would result from this or that decision.

It was in the nature of the new dispensation that the Representatives who had the care of the animals were now more important than any of us. Only down near the warm pole was it possible to grow crops, and these were of new cold-resistant varieties. We could not grow enough to feed people as much grain as once we did.

Our diet had changed, and very fast. The herds of enormous shaggy beasts who seemed to thrive on the new thin grasses and lichens gave us meat, gave us hides for clothing, provided us with cheeses and all kinds of soured milks that we had not before troubled to develop. A child was now weaned on to meat and cheeses: not long ago the diet would have been cooked grains—our food had been mostly fruit and cereals and vegetables. We wondered how this new way of eating might be affecting us. Canopus had the experience to tell us but Canopus had not been near us for some time. We would ask them . . .

The Animal Keepers and the Animal Makers called us all together to say that we were dependent on this one species of animal. We had learned—had we not?—how fast and thoroughly species could change . . . disappear . . . come into being. What guarantee had we that some new climatic shift might not kill off these new beasts of ours as quickly as the animals of our old time had been killed?

We were all together in one of our newly built places, thick walls around us, the roof heavy above. Very quiet our living had become, where we had been open to every breeze, every change of the light.

In this deep silence we sat together and measured our situation by how our responsibilities had changed.

The Representatives of the Representatives, of whom I was some-

times one, did not change their numbers. We were five, but sometimes we had other tasks as well. There was now one Grain Keeper
and Grain Maker. The Fruit and Vegetable Makers had become
Animal Makers, as I have suggested. The Food Makers had always
been the most necessary of our Makers and Keepers. Next to them,
those who built and cared for buildings. The numbers of these had
not lessened, but increased. Fifteen of our fifty now concerned
themselves with how to shelter our populations in this hard time.
There were the Maintainers of the Wall. The others were concerned with the making of implements and artefacts of all kinds,
some introduced by Canopus, others developed by us. Not long ago
we had one Representative for the Law. Now there were several,
because the tensions and difficulties made people quarrel where they
had been good-humoured. It had been, before The Ice, a rare thing
to have a killing. Now we expected murder. We had not thieved
from each other: now it was common. Once civic disobedience had
been unknown. Now gangs of mostly young people might roam
about throwing sticks and stones at anything that seemed to an-
tagonize them—often the base of the wall.

But this meeting was not concerned with anything but food. It
was necessary to discover, or make, or plan, new sources of food.

What had we overlooked, or deliberately left unused? There was
our ocean, filled with creatures of all sorts, but even now our
sense of the sacredness of the place made us reluctant to look at
it as a food source. I have to say that Canopus had never done more
than remain silent, when we talked of our Sacred Lake: this was
how they dealt with attitudes of ours they expected us to outgrow.
There were a few of us who long ago had come privately to think
that this sacredness and holiness was foolish, but we talked about
our thoughts only with each other. We had learned from Canopus
that argument does not teach children, or the immature. Only time
and experience does that.

So when some of our band of companions showed signs of emotion at the suggestion that our lake should be examined, we remained silent, as Canopus did at such times.

There remained only what we had turned our backs on and what
we so feared: the freezing wilderness. When we had made our

observation tours along the wall we had seen that the great birds we so loved to watch had become a snowy white, were no longer brown and grey. Wings soft and feathery and white as some kinds of snow now balanced on those hostile currents. Sometimes we might see a great many birds, but it was hard to pick them out against the snow masses, and often showers or storms filled the air so that birds and snow together whirled about the skies. But they must be feeding on something. . . . If we could not see any creatures on those white wastes, it did not mean they were not there.

It was decided to send a party of us to the cold pole, and I was chosen, because I had been to the other planets and had seen— though not from as close as this—landscapes of the cold. And two of the others had been on similar journeys. I, Doeg, Memory Maker and Keeper of Records, Klin who had once been our best Fruit Maker, and Marl who had been one of the Keepers of the Herds that had become extinct were the three who had been taken abroad by Canopus, and we were of those who sometimes found our companions overprone to simple emotions, as in the matter of our lake, and we had long been close friends. The other two were young, a boy and girl whose turn had come for apprenticeship. With us, reaching the age of qualifying for apprenticeship had been the occasions of festivals and rejoicing. It meant entry into adulthood. But now, with our once various and always expanding crafts and skills reduced, and with so much of what we had to learn to do difficult and dour and sometimes savage, there was little joy left and too few opportunities, and this journey of ours was seen by all our young as something marvellous: the competition was keen. Such were our fears that we were reluctant to choose the best, but we did in the end choose the best. Their names were Alsi and Nonni and they were brave good children, and they were beautiful. Or, would once have been: as things were, they huddled yellowly, as we did, inside what seemed to us like moving tents of thick clumsiness.

Our trouble was that we were not able to imagine the reality of the savagery of the cold. Not even though we had made brief trips into that region, not even though we searched our memories for anything we had learned of other planets and their means of dealing with extremes.

We put on to little sliding carts supplies of dried meat—which we all hated, though we were hungry enough for it; hide coats in case we lost or spoiled ours; and a sort of tent made of hides. We all thought this small provision would be enough to keep us safe.

We set out in a still morning, sliding down from our wall, not troubling about the steps, which were slippery and dangerous now, and falling into a drift from which we had to struggle. And we had to fight through waist-high feathery snow all that day, so that by nightfall we had not reached our objective: a certain hill in which we believed we would find a cave. Our sun, which seemed feeble enough these days, burned us by reflection and hurt our eyes. All around was white, white, white, and the skies soon filled with white snow masses and the whiteness was a horror and an agony, for nothing in our history as a race, and therefore nothing in our bodies or our minds, was prepared for it. The dark came down when we were in a vast field where the snow was light and soft and spun about and made plumes and eddies. Our tent could not find a hold, but kept sinking as if into water. We huddled together, opening our shaggy coats so as to press our bodies' warmth into each other, and our arms sheltered each other's necks and heads. That night there was no snow or storm, so we survived it, though we would not otherwise have done. In the morning we struggled on through the soft suffocating stuff, and then climbed up on to a glacier of hard ice which was so slippery that we made no quicker an advance, though it was better than the thick softness of the snow, into which we were afraid we would vanish altogether. On the ice we slipped and stumbled, but ignored our bruises and our aches, and that night reached the hill in which we knew was a cave. But the entrance to it was a sheet of ice. We were able to put up our tent in a hollow where snow lay. It was made of ten of the largest hides stitched together, with the pelts inwards, and we laid down more hides on the ice, and huddled there till morning. We were not as cold as the night before, but the shaggy fell of the inside of the tent was soaked with the moisture from our bodies and in the morning it was solid ice—stiff rods and points of ice that threatened to cut us as we wriggled out, face down, into the new day, which was clear and free of cloud.

We had begun to understand how little we were prepared for this journey, and I for one wanted to give it up. We three older ones all wanted to turn back, but the two youngsters pleaded with us, and we gave in. We were shamed by them—not so much by their brave and shining eyes, their dauntlessness, but by something more subtle. When a generation watches the young ones, their future, their responsibility, grow up, and when what they are to inherit is pitiful and so reduced, then the shame of it goes too deep for reasoning. No, it was not our fault that our children had to learn such hardship, had to forego so much that we, the older ones, had inherited. Our fault it was not; but we *felt* that it was. We were learning, we old ones, that in times when a species, a race, is under threat, drives and necessities built into the very substance of our flesh speak out in ways that we need never have known about if extremities had not come to squeeze these truths out of us. An older, a passing, generation needs to hand on goodness, something fine and high—even if it is only in potential—to their children. And if there isn't this bequest to put into their hands, then there is a bitterness and a pain that makes it hard to look into young eyes, young faces.

We, the three Representatives, agreed to go on.

Because the skies were clear and blue on that third day we could see the great white birds everywhere, floating over the snows and the ice, looking downwards for—what prey? At first we could see nothing, but then, straining our eyes against the glare, did see small movements that seemed to creep and run in a way different from the smoke and the surge of snows moved by the wind. And then we saw little black specks on the white, and they were droppings; and then larger pieces that were the droppings of the white birds, which had in them fur and bones, and from these we were able to form some picture of the little snow animals before we actually saw one: we were on it, it was under our feet, and it rolled over in a pleading confiding way as if in play. A sort of rodent, completely white, with soft blue eyes. And once we had seen them we were able to pick them out, running around, though not very many—certainly not to be seen as a food supply. Unless they could be bred in captivity? But what were they feeding on? We saw one eating the droppings of the big birds . . . if the birds ate them, and they ate their own remnants in the birds' droppings, then this was a closed cycle and hardly feasible—but there seemed nothing available for them to eat. We did see a few, a very few, snow-beetles, or some kind of insect, white too—but what did *they* feed on, if they were the food of the little white beasts?

As we planned to travel polewards for several days yet, we did not capture specimens but pressed on. Ahead I knew was a range of hills and in them some deep caves, and we hoped they would not be completely iced in. On an afternoon when the sky was a metallic dark-blue glare, we slid and staggered our way up a river that we knew was one only because we had enjoyed it when it ran between green fertile banks and was crowded with boats and swimmers. The sides now rose sheer up, cliffs of ice. To reach the place of the caves we had to cut steps in the ice, and the boy Nonni fell and hurt his arm very badly, though he pretended not to be much hurt.

Although it would soon be dark and we wanted very much to be sheltered, we had to give him time to recover. We sat down in a hollow in the ice, with our backs to the cliff and looking out over a coldly brilliant scene: a sharp blue sky that seemed to us cruel, defining the dead white of the landscape. We were breathing shallowly and as little as we could because each breath hurt our lungs. Our limbs ached. Our eyes kept trying to close themselves. Yet we knew that what we felt was nothing compared to the pain that made Nonni sit cramped there, breathing at long intervals in great gasps, his eyes seeing nothing of the vivid blue and white and dazzle around us. He was not far from slipping off into unconsciousness, and Alsi put her arms around him from behind, carefully because of his broken elbow, or shoulder—we could not tell what was broken, because of the mass of clothing—and she enclosed him in her vitality and her strength. To us three watching, the contrast between the two young faces was a warning: hers, in spite of what she had to endure, so alive and commanding, his all drowse and yellow indifference.

"Nonni," she began, in what was at once evident to us as a deliberate attempt to rouse him, "Nonni, wake up, talk to us, you must keep awake, you must talk . . ."

And, as his face showed the peevishness and irritation of his reluctance, she persisted, "No, no, Nonni, I want you to talk. You lived near here, didn't you? Didn't you? Come on, tell us!" He shifted his head from side to side, and then turned it away from the pressure of her cheek on his, but his eyes opened and there was consciousness in them: he understood what she was doing for him.

"Where did you live?"

He indicated with a weak lift of his head, which at once fell back against her shoulder, that it was somewhere there in front of us.

"And how? And what did you do?"

"You know what I did!"

"Go on!"

Again he resisted her, with an involuntary movement that said he wanted only to slide away into sleep, but she would not let him, and he gasped out: "Before The Ice, it was there—there."

There was now the plain of snow, undulating, cut by crevasses and sending up small eddies and whirls of snow.

"And you lived in a town down there, and it was one of our largest towns, and people used to come from all over the planet to visit it, because it was the only town like it? A new kind of town?"

He struggled to evade her with irritable shiftings of his head, shutting his eyes, but again his will to live came back.

"The town was built there because these hills are full of iron. Under the ice here are the mine workings. A road goes from here to there—the best road on the planet, because of what it had to carry, heavy loads of ore, from which we made trucks to carry even more ore . . ."

Here he seemed to drowse again, and Alsi said: "Please, Nonni."

"Before our town was built and we began mining, there was no centre for making iron, though it was made in a small way everywhere. It was Canopus who told us to look for iron here, and what to look for, and then how to work it and mix it with other metals. It was clear to us that these metals we were making would change the way we all lived. Some people did not like what was happening.

Some left our town again and went to live in other places where life had not changed."

"And you, did you like it?"

"It seems that I must have, because I was going to be a worker in metals, like my parents. Both of them knew all the new processes. Just before The Ice I travelled with them, to a town not far from our ocean, and it was the first time I had seen anything different."

"And how did it seem?" said Alsi, teasing him, for she knew.

"It seemed to me charming," he said, full again of the youthful scornfulness he had felt, so that we all laughed, and he laughed too, since now he was able to look back and see himself. "Yes, it was so *pretty*, and so *soft*. With us everything was so much harder. Every day we had a new invention or discovery, and we were learning to make metals we hadn't ever thought of. It seemed as if something quite new had happened to us, and we could not help but make new things and have new ideas. After that visit, I was glad to get back. And Canopus came again about then. Because we had seen how differently people lived in other parts of the planet, and we could make comparisons, we asked Canopus how things were on other planets. And suddenly our minds seemed filled with newness . . . we were stretched . . . we were much larger than we had been . . . we knew how many different ways there were of living, we talked about how species began and grew and changed—and died out . . ." Here he stopped for a moment and was silent, a darkness coming over his face.

"Nonni, we are not going to die out, Canopus says so."

"Some of us will not," he said, in a direct statement of something he felt, something he knew, and it chilled us. We knew then, or at least we older ones did, that Nonni would not survive.

"That was the real change, it seems to me now. Not only that because we were making new metals and all kinds of machines we knew life on our planet would change, but because for the first time we thought in this way at all—and then began to think about how many different ways of living there could be—and then, of course, it followed that we wondered if we could choose how we would develop, choose the direction we would go in. . . . It seems now as if what really happened for the first time was the idea of choice. . . . And then there was The Ice!" And he laughed out strongly, an angry laugh, as only the very young can laugh. The anger injected energy into him, and he staggered up, and was supported by Alsi. "What are we doing sitting here? Look, the light is going. We should get under cover."

It was he who led the way up while we followed, watching him so that we could hold him if he slipped. But his strength held out until we got to shelter, though it was the last real effort he was able to make for himself.

We found under a deep overhang of blue ice a part-frozen dirt shelf, and behind that a cave with a soft dirt floor—and so long did it already seem to us since we had seen earth that we handled it with affection and in need for reassurance. Touching it released odours, and we knew that this was guano, or droppings, and looking up thought we would see bats, but there were none, they had been killed by the cold. Yet in this cave, with the unfrozen dirt beneath our feet, there was something that disturbed us, made us look continually over our shoulders.

We spread out our pelts on the cave floor, and lit a big fire in the entrance, using the guano as fuel; and when the flames leaped up, and the smoke began to eddy, we heard a stirring in the heart of the cave, as if creatures were alerted, and were withdrawing farther and deeper. We kept vigil all that night, though in the comparative warmth of the place we all found it easy to sleep. We each took a watch, and all felt that a watch was being kept on us— we had a sense of being stared at. In the morning, we felt the lack of something that it had not occurred to us to supply ourselves with. We needed a torch. There was no branch or stick or anything that would make a torch. The daylight fell only a little way into the cave. All five of us, in a strong close group, went as far into the cave as we dared, and knew that not far from us were living beings. We sensed a mass of living warmth. Many small things? A few large ones? And if large, what? The vegetation-eaters of our lost time could not have survived.

Did the little snow rodents mass in what caves still were free of the ice packs? Did the great birds nest in caves? Was there some other kind of bird or animal we had not imagined?

It was with feelings of loss, even of anguish, that we left those creatures behind: this was because, of course, we identified with them. How could we not, pressed in upon as we were, so that our lives became ever smaller and narrower? We could feel for these poor animals, whatever they were, surviving in an icebound cave.

We travelled on polewards, but more slowly because of Nonni's bad arm. He could not help with pulling the sliding carts, and Alsi did his work. And then we lost our sense of time, and of distance, as we laboured on, and on; our eyes burning, the exposed skin of our faces painful, and even the bones of our bodies protesting— those light elegant bones of ours that had been made by nature for easy and graceful movement. Over us storms came down, and we were enclosed in shrieking winds that never stopped, until we came to believe that a screaming of air in violent movement was what was normal, and silence or the soft stirrings of breezes and zephyrs only what we made ourselves imagine to save our reason from present horror. And then, when the storms stopped, and we found newly deposited snows preventing our struggling progress forwards, and the snow masses fled past overhead, our space in the world seemed shrunk to no more than our group of shivering bodies, so that we were in a white room whose walls pressed in on us as we moved and that moved with us. And when the skies lifted and cleared, and we were in a high valley surrounded by tall icy peaks, there was no life but in ourselves, our few small selves huddled together there. Again we could not put up our tent on the hard ice. Night came down on us and we did not sleep, for the wonder and the splendour and the terror of the place. Overhead a black sky, with a few brilliant stars. No wind, no clouds, only silence. We crouched there, trembling, and gazed up, at this bright star and then at another, asking if this was the sun of Rohanda, the fruitful planet, or if that was; and we talked of the race that Canopus was bringing up to a level of high evolution, and we wondered how these people, who in our imaginations had everything brave and strong and good in them, would welcome us and make us at home . . . and we talked of how we two races, these nurslings of Canopus and ourselves, who were also the children of Canopus, their creation, would work together, and live together and become even stronger and better. And we, the three older ones, were aware of the vibrant expectation and longing of the two young ones, and we felt for them all the warm protective love that a passing generation must feel for its charges.

How still it was through that long night, and how beautiful! The silence was so deep we could hear the small crystalline whispering of the stars. And, before dawn, when the cold was so intense our thick fleecy coats seemed to have crumbled away, leaving us naked, one of the high glittering peaks that surrounded us let out a violent cracking noise, as the icy blast bit into it, and this sound was echoed by another peak, and in a moment all the mountains seemed to be shouting and groaning and protesting with the cold. And then it was silent again, and the stars sparkled and invited. We did not believe we would survive that night, and in the first light that made everything glitter and hurt our eyes we found Nonni slow and heavy, and we pushed back the shags of fur from around his face so we could see the truth of his state: and his flesh was thin and yellow and clung to his bones, and his dark eyes had no answer in them. We were still a good way from the pole. I remembered that there had been a cave not far from here, and we carried him to it. He was so light he lay in my arms like a child. The cave had a small entrance, a hole in the snow; and there was no guano there. The floor was a hard greyish mixture of soil and frost, and we had no sense of animals watching from the cave's recesses. We found piles of straw from—we supposed—the habitation of a solitary or a hermit, and with this we made a bit of a fire. But there was not enough warmth to save Nonni, and he died. And we could not bury him, for the floor was too hard. We left him there, in his thick pelts, and we four, wondering which of us would be next, went on with this journey of ours that we believed useless and perhaps even criminal, until we saw ahead of us a tall black spiring thing. It was the column that Canopus had asked us to erect at the place of the pole. But it was not as high as we remembered it, for the ice had reached more than half the way up it. The columns were at the poles because the spacecraft of Canopus found them useful as markers when they came in to land.

It seemed to us that the sun here at the top of our world was hotter than anywhere on our journey. It will be remembered that I said there was the very slightest inclination of our planet on its axis, which had never been enough to make much difference in our good times; but now we wondered if perhaps, because we were in such extremities of climate, this small slant might make enough of a change to call it a summer, when the other pole in its turn reached forward closer to the sun. Well, it turned out that it was so: there was the briefest season of weather when a slight increase in warmth made it possible to bring on crops and cosset a few vegetables. But it could not be summer enough to change our situation.

Here at the top of the planet, with nothing around us but glazed ice on which we could hardly keep our footing, we had to acknowledge that we had not found anything that could be of use as foodstock, except perhaps the white snow creatures. Which did not live up here, in these latitudes—here nothing lived. And our small livingness, our slow and cold-confused thoughts seemed to us out of place, almost an affront to nature which had ordained only the silences of the ice, the shrieking of the storms.

On the way back, the girl fell ill and we had to pull her along on one of the carts—there was room for her, now we had eaten nearly all our dried meat. When we reached the valleys, where the small movement of the snow animals showed on the snows among the shadows of the great birds that swung their white wings overhead, we caught several. This was easy, for they did not know enough to fear us. They were confiding little beasts, and snuggled up to the girl who lay half-conscious on her bed, and their sweetness and warmth revived her, and she wept for the first time, because of the death of her friend Nonni.

Of the journey back there is no need to say any more than it was frightful, and every dragging and painful step told us how foolish we had been to match ourselves against dangers we had not been equipped to measure. When at last we reached where we expected to see our black wall, we did not see it. It was a blindingly brilliant glittering morning, after a night of snow that fell so heavily we thought we might be suffocated by it. Stumbling on, our eyes half-closed against the glare, we nearly stepped straight over a cliff—our wall; we had walked up to it at the level of its top, for ice and snow had filled in everything. Standing there and looking down, we could see that snow had been blown down from the cold side into drifts along the foot of the wall. Not deep drifts, but enough to cover the earth to a good distance.

We climbed carefully down the slippery dangerous steps into safety. Alsi soon recovered, and she took the little beasts that had shared her cart with her to the Animal Makers, and at last, after much experimentation, it was found they would eat lichens and the low bushes of the tundras. But what had they lived on when they were in that wilderness of frozen water? It was at last decided that in the caves there must have been supplies of straw or leaves, or perhaps even some sort of vegetation growing. We bred these creatures for food; but our problem was, after all, that we were not able to grow enough to feed animals. The great herds, which had seemed able to thrive on such sparse and dry vegetation, were now roaming restlessly from valley to hillside and even up the mountains in search of food. If the cold was going to creep down past our barrier wall, then we must expect our grasses and shrubs to dwindle—and the herds to dwindle too.

It was this pressure on us that made our more tender-minded Representatives agree to think again about our lake. Our ocean. A ceremony was made of it. All the populations of the valleys round about, and delegations from every part of our planet, stood along the edges of our ocean. It was a sombre, grey morning, and the crowds were silent and grey. From where we stood on the low hills on one side of the stretch of water, we could see a greyish brown huddling of people around the far shores. We Representatives were on the shore nearest the wall, and we could see, far over the mountains on the other side of the water, a light greyish blue sky that seemed still to smile. Populations under threat know silences that they understand nothing of in lighthearted times. The people around me could be observed turning their faces about, to look into other faces; all were silent, or speaking only in very low voices, and it came into my mind that the reason for this deep attentiveness was because they were, we all were, *listening*. Everything we had to do was difficult and hateful to us, we were not at ease with even the smallest and most ordinary and often-repeated things in our daily lives, from the putting on of the heavy coats to the preparing of the fatty meat which was our staple food; not at ease in our sleep that was always threatened by cold creeping in from somewhere, a heavy weight of cold that seemed to subside into us, like water soaking clay; not at ease even in the stretching out of a hand or a smile, for our bodies and faces seemed always too light and friable for what they had to do and had to express. There seemed to be nothing left to us that was instinctive and therefore joyful, or ordinarily pleasurable. We were foreign to ourselves as much as to our surroundings. And therefore groups, and crowds, sank easily and often into silences. As if this sense, hearing, was being pressed into service in default of other senses which we needed and lacked. We *listened*—the eyes of every one of us had in them always a look of waiting to hear or receive some news, or message or information.

There had been some of us Representatives who had said that we ought to make of this occasion, the dedicating of our lake to usefulness and productivity, a ceremony of songs and chants, contrasting the bleakness of our present time with the past. The so recent past . . . it was only the young children there who did not remember our lake set blue and bright among the greens and yellows of foliage. What need of a formal ritual of memory? Our stretch of shining waters had been blue, and had been green, and there had been little white wavelets on it. Brown rocks had made diving places all around the amazingly and improbably coloured shores . . . living always in dun and grey and dirt colour, the hues of a warmed and fruitful land come to seem extraordinary, almost impossible. Had we stood here, we people of our stricken planet—stood here and looked at lively brown bodies diving and swimming in sky-reflecting waters? We had danced and sung around these shores on warm nights when these soft dark waters had seemed crammed with stars? We *had?* Well, we knew we had, and we told our younger children about it all . . . and their eyes, puzzling at our faces, said they believed it all as they believed the legends we had been given by Canopus to repeat to them. For Canopus had told us Representatives a thousand tales that would prepare the minds of our people for understanding our role as a planet among planets, and how we were cherished and fed and watched over by Canopus. I myself remember how, as a small child, I was taken out on to a hillside by the Representatives of that time, with other children, on a soft warm night, and shown how a certain brilliant star, low on the horizon, was Canopus, our fostering and nurturing star. I remember how I fought with my own mind to take it all in, how I matched the rustling of the grasses around me, the familiar warmth of my parents' hands, and the pleasant smell of their flesh, with the thought: that shining thing up there, that little shine, is a world, like ours, like our planet here, and I must remember when I look at that star that it is a world, and my Maker.

I remember how I part-understood, partially accepted. And how the legends and tales sank into my mind and fed it, and made in me a place that I could enter at will, to refresh myself, and to feed myself with largeness and wholeness. But it had not been easy, that slow change, monitored always (as I knew, though with difficulty) by Canopus.

What our task was that cold day looking out across the grey water was to hear from each other, and to understand, that this sacredness, this untouched wonder of a place, which we had swum in and played in but never never desecrated—was now to be farmed as we had once farmed nearly all the planet. As we still did farm the small area around the pole that was thrust forward—slightly, only very slightly—into our sun's fruitful light. Yes, we were making use of our slight, almost imperceptible "summer." We would harvest from our "ocean" the creatures in it, but carefully, for there were many of us, and not so many of them that we could take as much as we liked.

The Representatives for the Keeping of the Lake, its Guardians, named Rivalin, stood forth from the silent crowds, and got into a boat that was decorated and made as cheerful as we could contrive with our now so limited resources of vegetation—some garlands made of lichens, and stalks of grain—and sailed out a little way from our chilly shores, and stood there on the deck, holding up the new instruments, for all to see. They were nets, and all kinds of lines with hooks, and spears and harpoons. These last were because there were tales that deep in the centre of our lake were monsters. Sometimes people had drowned, though not often, and it was said they had been taken down into the deeps of the lake by these great creatures no one had ever seen. And which never had existed—or at least, we never saw them.

Something happened when the Representatives lifted up the new weapons, high above their heads, and turned them around to show us. A groan or cry came out from the crowds, and this sound, which had been pressed out of us, frightened us all. There were moments of wild lament. For what? Because our necessity made us violate what had previously been sacred to us? It was not only on our shore that this wild groaning cry rose up from the people. All around the edges of the lake, people had gone out in boats with the implements of catching the creatures of the water, and from every shore had come this keening dirge.

And when the brief moment of the lament was over, there was silence again, the deep listening silence.

Some of the people waited to see the first creatures being drawn from the water. We had of course seen these often enough, while swimming there. It was while observing them, the long narrow agile water creatures, shaped rather like birds without wings—though some seemed to use frail and small wings—that we had first been inspired to think about how creatures took the shape of their environment, were the visible maps or charts of what they lived in. Birds, both the solitary individualists of our new time, and the lively flocks of the old time, traced for us the currents of the air. And these water beasts, the lone ones, who seemed always to be the larger, and those who moved and swerved and fled about in flocks or crowds or shoals, expressed visibly the currents of the liquid which we could not see, any more than we could the movements of the air. The running, swirling, rolling, and spiralling of air and water would become evident to us as we watched their creatures.

But most of the people made their way home. We Representatives stood on a rise and watched these poor people, our charges, go quickly, almost furtively, as if they were afraid of being watched, or even criticised, into their dwellings. Criticised for what? In times of great calamity, it is unfortunately true that populations feel guilty. Guilty of what? Ah, but what is the use of such rational, such cool, questioning when faced with the sudden, improbable, unexpected afflictions of nature! Our populations felt as if they were being punished . . . yet they had done no wrong . . . yet this was what they felt. We had only to look at them to see it—how they moved and stood and searched each other's faces for confirmation or reassurance. When they stood, it was as if an invisible burden rested on them, making them hunch their shoulders, and giving an obdurate suffering look to the way they held their heads. They huddled together, and they walked glancing about them as if enemies lurked. Yet we had never had enemies. We had not known, until recently, even common crime or criminals. These people, these fortunate happy peoples, so recently blithe and agile and impulsive and trusting of each other and of the earth they lived in and on— they now could not make a gesture or a movement without expressing not only fear, but a wrong—and this was a wrong deep in themselves.

We had discussed how to remedy this: if we should appeal, talk to them, explain, argue, reason . . . Why should you, our brave and gallant peoples, facing so well and with such courage these hard times that have changed so terribly everything we all knew— why should you look as if you had been condemned to atone for a crime? No crime has been committed! You are not at fault! Please, do not make worse for yourselves and for each other what is already bad enough. Please, think of how this new posture or stance of yours, as if at each moment you expect a judge to pronounce sentence on you, must be undermining you, eating away in all of us, in our deepest beings . . .

Thus the voice of reason. As we envisaged using it. But did not use it. Reason cannot reach the springs of unreason, to cure or heal them. No, something much deeper in cause and source than we, the Representatives, could come near, was working in our peoples.

And of course in us too, for we were of them and in them. Therefore, of necessity, we too were being afflicted, if not at the level we could see so easily in our peoples, then perhaps somewhere deeper and even perhaps worse? How could we know? How could we choose rightly what to do and to say when we had to suspect what was going on in our own minds, had to be wary of our judgment?

What could we conceivably find to say strong enough to outweigh what everybody had to live with day and night: this knowledge that because of events unknown to us, certain movements of the stars (cosmic forces, as Canopus phrased it, though these words did nothing to lessen our bewilderment) were causing our Home Planet, the lovely Planet 8, to wither and die. Nothing we could do or think or say might change this basic truth, and we all had to live with it as we were able, facing perils we did not understand. But, in the future, in some distant time, or perhaps a near time, for we did not know what to expect, Canopus would come and take us all off to Rohanda the fruitful, Rohanda the temperate and the welcoming.

We did go off, we Representatives, to our meeting place, and we sat together, for the rest of that day. Sat mostly in silence. Once we had met in the open air, on a hillside, or at night under stars. Now we sat close together, with our coats kept on, under a low roof. It was very cold. We did not use fires or heating by then: any vegetable matter, or dung, or lichens, or even the earth which can be slowly burned, had to be thought of now in terms of possible feed for animals. We had observed the great herds, in their frenzied search for enough to eat, pawing up this earth that was half vegetable matter, and eating it, though they disliked it, and often spat it out. But then they took it up into their mouths again.

When the Representatives who had been floating around the edges of the lake showing the new methods for catching food came in and sat with us, we discussed how best to use this new resource.

I shall simply say here that while the food in the lake did do something to soften our hard lot, it wasn't much, wasn't enough. While our populations could not be described as large, compared to those of some planets which we knew were numbered in millions, they were not small enough to be fed long from a moderate-sized lake. And while this food was valued by us, we did not enjoy it. How we hungered and longed for the vegetables and fruits and grains of our old diet . . . all our food was animal now, unless we scraped lichens from the rocks. We were coarsening because of it, becoming thickset, and with a greasy heavy look, so that it was hard to remember what we had been once. Even our skins seemed to be dulling into the prevailing grey, grey, grey that we could see everywhere. Grey skies, a grey or brownish earth, greyish green covering on the rocks, greyish dun herds, and the great birds overhead grey and brown . . . though more and more, when they came floating over the wall, which was grey now because of the frost that had it in its grip, they were white . . . light white feathery floating birds, from the white wastes beyond our barrier wall.

When we looked up at that wall, we could see how the ice had come pressing down and over its top. A dirty greyish white shelf projected from our wall: it was the edge of a glacier. If the wall gave, then what could stand between us and the ice and snow of that interminable winter up there, whose shrieking winds and gales kept us awake at nights, while we huddled together under the mounds of thick hides? But the wall would not give. It could not . . . Canopus had prescribed it, Canopus had ordered it. Therefore, it would stand . . .

But where was Canopus?

If we were to be rescued in time for our peoples to be saved, then that time was already past.

I have said that new crimes and violences afflicted us. The victims were not many, but each crime seemed to us an enormity, and appalling, simply because we had not known this before.

It is not easy to allot grief or self-reproach fairly and properly in this business of calamity, when it affects people so variously and insidiously. That the individual victims of a murder or a casual looting made us more uneasy and angry than when twenty people died because of a sudden snowstorm was not *reasonable*. Was it because we felt we were responsible for the violence, even though there had been no violence or acts of terror before this new time of nature's cruelty to us? Looked at like that, no one was to blame for these killings, which were, obviously, part of the general worsening of everything. Once any death was a public grief, and a genuine one. We knew each other. It was not possible for a face to be unknown, even if names were.

But the change had begun some time back: when Nonni died in the cold, we did not suffer very much. We were too cold and too threatened ourselves. Alsi mourned for him, but not as she might have done once. No, death had a new quality, and one that made us ashamed. We could not care as once we had . . . that was the truth of it. Was it that the cold was chilling our hearts, slowing our blood, making us less loving and responsive to each other? A child died, and we all knew we might be thinking secretly: So much the better; what horrors is it going to be spared, this unfortunate one! Almost certainly more fortunate than we the survivors! And we knew we were thinking: One less mouth to feed. And: It would be better if children were not born at all, not in this terrible time. And, as I have already suggested, when a species begins to think like this about its most precious, its original, capacity, that of giving birth, of passing on an inheritance, then it is afflicted indeed. If we are not channels for the future, and if this future is not to be better than we are, better than the present, then what are we?

We knew what we had been: and, as the news came in of riots in another valley, food riots, or perhaps even for no apparent cause, then we looked up into our dreary skies and thought: *Canopus, when are you coming, when will you fulfil your promise to us?*

Then Canopus came, but not as we had expected. A great fleet of her spaceships floated in by way of the warm pole, and landed on our tundras; and what seemed an army of Canopeans unloaded supplies from the ships. We did not at first know what they all were, for we were rejoicing over foodstuffs we had not seen for so long—all kinds of dried and preserved fruits and vegetables. But mostly there were mountains of containers with some sort of pliable substance, and the Canopeans said they were for insulating our dwellings.

Were they not bearers of some other message? Nothing from Johor, for instance? Were we not to be given a time for our being finally rescued?

No, nothing of that kind—the space-fleet had been ordered to bring in these materials, and this is what had been done. And with that, the craft lifted up again into the skies and vanished.

The material for covering our houses was new to us. It was very thick soft easily manipulated stuff, and what we had to do was to make of it shells and hoods and coats for our dwellings. So light was this material that it was easy for a few people to cut, to fit together, and then to lift these shells over the buildings. We debated whether to cut windows in each carapace, but decided not to. For ventilation we had to rely on the opening and shutting of doors. Inside our homes now we crowded in a dark which was lit dimly by electricity that we supplemented when we could by lichen moulds soaked in tallow. Our world was now dark, dark, and always darker as the skies overhead became thicker and greyer. We woke in the stuffy dark that was warmed a little because of the press of bodies, and lit our little glimmers of light, or allowed ourselves the weakest trickle of electricity; and we went out into a world that showed a trace of brightness and light only far down towards the pole, where sometimes there was a little blue. From over the grey wall came driving the snow-laden winds. Now snow flurries played and smoked around the foot of our side of the wall, and tempests were common. And each bout of screaming winds seemed to drive us deeper down against the earth. Not all our buildings had been covered over with the insulating material. In some of our towns were buildings of as many as five or even six layers of function. (I am aware of course that this will seem unimpressive to those of you who live on planets where buildings may be as tall as cliffs and mountains. I have seen such buildings myself.) These were too tall for us to be able to cover them over. Some hardy persons had elected to remain in them, but every storm emptied layer after layer, leaving perhaps a few people on the ground layer or on the one above that. And those who had been driven out of their high unprotected dwellings and working places massed together lower down, then were driven by force of numbers into joining families or groups or clans who perhaps had slightly more room than others. Thus adding to the overcrowding . . . to the tensions . . . to the always worsening moods and tempers of everybody. Rapidly worsening: having to put the heavy coverings over our living places had seemed to bring us all to a sudden new pitch of explosiveness. From everywhere came the news of the evidences of it.

"There has been fighting on the other side of the planet."

"Fighting? Has someone been killed?"

"Many. Very many."

"Many people have been killed? Why, did so many quarrels break out all at the same time?"

"You see, groups of people have been fighting."

"Fighting against each other? Groups?"

"Yes, groups, the people of one village fought another."

"But what for?"

"Each village accused the other of the same bad behaviour."

"I don't understand!"

Yes, that is how the news of our first battles was received by us. And this incomprehension persisted.

"They are fighting between the mountains over there."

"Fighting? Who? What for? Have we been invaded, then? Have enemies come from the skies?"

"No, no, the people in the land just past those foothills, you remember, where our young people used to journey to look for wives and husbands."

"How can they be fighting! What about?"

And then it was: "They are at war in the next valley."

"War?"

"Yes, the villages there have divided themselves into two factions and are permanently armed against each other."

"Has anyone been killed?"

And so it went on. For a long time. Went on even when something of the kind happened among ourselves. Families that had been braving it out on the ground level of one of the unprotected buildings found that snow had covered the apertures; and they emerged and went from one to another of the neighbouring dwellings—and were turned away. Were refused in one place after another. Until they took up weapons of all kinds, stones, and sticks, and even the implements used for killing the creatures of the lake, and forced their way into a habitation. There they stayed, a hostile and defensive clan, in one part of the dwelling, setting watchers to report the first sign of hostile retaliation. They slept and cooked food and went about their lives as a unit; and they were in a large room separated from their enemies by a single wall. And these threatened ones came with weapons to throw them out, and did succeed in expelling them. And again the homeless clan went from one place to another, trying to force entrance. Scuffling and fighting went on, all around the different dwellings, in a thick snowfall, which made it hard for them to see who were enemies and who friends. Then when they forced entrance, the invaders and invaded fought in the dimness and the dark of the interior spaces. We Representatives were sent for. The Representative for Housing and Sheltering went in to them, and insisted on the clan breaking itself up into ones and twos, and dispersed them among many households. We had not before had to divide a clan, let alone a family. We all understood this to be a new descent for us into unpleasantness and even danger. For the clan was our basic unit, and we felt it as our strength, our foundation as a people. Yet there was no alternative. We could not build new dwelling places. We did not have the materials. We could only make the best use of those we had.

It was not only the dispersal of some clans that threatened us in a new way. There was almost a rebellion: the clan had obeyed the Representative, but only just. Very easily could they have refused. We did not have the means to enforce our will on others. We had never thought of ourselves as separate from them. We had not envisaged having to make individuals or groups do what they bitterly resisted. Our strength was all in our election by them, to fulfil what we all knew was a general will, a consensus. If there was no agreement we could not function. If this group had said to our Representative: No, we will not! then there was nothing we could have done. It would have been the end of our way of life as a people.

We all knew that. And the fear of general anarchy was what, in the end, made the intruding clan agree to dissolve itself and go quietly off, though not willingly, to new households.

It was a time, still, that soon we would look back on as one of innocence, when we had not known our good fortune.

But our main concern was not for the worsening temper of our people, but for the threat from the ice, which groaned and squealed as the thickening masses bore down towards us, piling up above the wall so that it seemed to us we looked up at a mountain that was moving. We Representatives went together to a place near the wall where there was a gap in the shelf of ice above, and we climbed carefully up steps that were crumbling and dangerous. The surface of the wall was friable, and was cracking minutely into a frosty crumble that we could rub loose under our fingers. But that was only the surface—so we hoped. One of us did slip and fall, almost from the top, but the drifts now were deep, and there was no harm done. The steps opened into a small space between tongues of ice that thrust forward on either side of us, and there we clustered and clung together, for it was hard to stand. And a bitter wind whined around us, spinning small crumbs of white so that all the air was thickened, and we could not see to the horizon. Below us our little town that had once shone whitely among green parks and avenues was now hard to map, for the grey sheltering hoods merged with the tundra so that we were looking down at an agglomeration of humps and protuberances that seemed as if the earth had grown them. Some of the taller buildings stood up sharp and dark, but the upper parts had collapsed in the blizzards, and had a splintered appearance. There were only small movements in the streets; few of the people went out of their dwellings now unless they had to. They had become a passive huddling population, sullen with in- activity, sullenly patient. They were waiting.

They waited for the moment when we would all be swept up and away from our dour frigid land to the paradise of Rohanda. Crouching inside low, dark, ill-smelling buildings, where all effort had become slowed and difficult with the cold, they waited. And, standing high there on that ice cliff above them, we peered through the dim skies and searched for Canopus, for the wonderful space- ships of our Saviour and Maker Canopus.

Where was Canopus? Why did they delay so, and make us wait and suffer and wonder, and doubt our survival? Make us disbelieve in ourselves and in them? What was the reason for it? Yes, they had warned us, and made us prepare ourselves, and they had prescribed our barrier wall, and they had taught us how to change our habits—it seemed sometimes as if this was a change to our very beings, our inner selves—and they had flown in this amazing substance that could clothe towns as if they were people. But we were *not* saved, not being rescued; and everywhere our peoples degenerated and became thieves and sometimes murderers, and there seemed no end to it all.

We voiced what we were thinking, that shivering morning, up on the ice cliff, we Representatives . . . fifty of us there were, and every activity or duty or work that we did (that was left to us now) was delineated there, by us. And as we stood there, looking into faces that were only just visible behind deep edges of shaggy fur, we could see the manifold purposes and uses of the old time, where now was—over and over again—Representative for Housing and Sheltering, Representative for Food, Representative for Conserving Warmth. And variations on these basic needs.

For we were keeping, and in a conscious effort, our knowledge of our own possibilities, our potential for the future, which had been so amply demonstrated in the past. We were *not* merely these shivering animals, concerned only with how to keep ourselves warm, keep ourselves fed—not just what we could see as we huddled there, trying to keep our footing as the wind tugged and shoved at us. No, we were still what we had been, and would be again . . . and where was Canopus, who would restore us to ourselves?

Again we made the journey around our planet, this time at the foot of the wall or cliff, not on it, as this was no longer possible because of its load of pressing ice. We stumbled through snow-drifts or over frozen earth, and our eyes were turned always to the right, for we kept the sun in front of us as much as we could—our poor weakened pallid sun which seemed now almost to be absorbing heat from us, rather than warming and nurturing us. Our eyes were at work at every moment on the surface of the wall, or cliff, for we feared very much that it would give way altogether. But so far, while every little part of it was crazed and crumbling, there were no large cracks in it. It was holding. This journey took us twice as long as when we had travelled with Canopus, and we were cold and torpid, and felt the need to sleep. Sleep . . . sleep . . . our minds found refuge there, and the need to lose ourselves in oblivion was a torment. We would sit pressed together, as soon as the light went, in some place where the snowdrifts were not so deep, with our backs to the great barrier, and we ate our tasteless and disagreeable dried meat, or roots of the half-frozen rushes: and we dozed there as if we were one organism, not many—as if our separate unique individualities had become another burden that had to be shed, like unnecessary movement. Yet we were in movement . . . alone of our peoples we felt some kind of restlessness, which had made us take this journey. While they dozed and dreamed away this long waiting time heaped together in their dark and frigid homes, we were still feeling a need to press on from place to place, as if elsewhere we could come on something that might aid us.

It was on that journey, while we huddled together as the light went, that one of us—Marl, he who had once been the expert breeder of now extinct animals—did not settle down immediately with the rest of us, but piled a snowdrift higher with his hands, making a windbreak that would save us from some discomfort. Marl had always been a strong and well-built man, and even now was able to move with some lightness and purpose, his movements precise, a pleasure to watch. We were watching: saw in that face, thinned as all our faces were, a concentration and an effort that brought us all up again to our feet—to determination, to self-discipline. And that night and the succeeding nights we all built walls, which grew higher, so that we sheltered deep inside a circle of piled snow that grew inwards at its top; and soon we spent our nights inside domes of packed snow. These on calmer nights remained firm above and around us, but when the blizzards came they blew away into the storm. And so we learned to pack the snow hard into massive pieces and piled them up; and knew that we had found a way of making some kind of dwelling for our homeless ones, who could not any longer stay in the tall buildings, and who were so unwelcome in the overcrowded households. Masson, the chief of the Representatives for Housing and Sheltering, was at work throughout the journey, mostly with Marl, packing snow this way and that way, using chunks of ice as strengtheners, experimenting with apertures and placing them high and low—finally making short tunnels that we crept along into the snowhouses, so that our bodies' heat would not be wasted.

So that journey accomplished more than only making sure our wall still stood firm and whole. And we were reminded that effort of one kind often brings as a reward accomplishments and knowledge that have not been envisaged at all. And we returned to our various hometowns and settlements with the determination to rouse our torpid peoples to effort—effort almost of any sort.

I, and Marl, and Klin, he who had once brought into being so many delightful varieties of fruit, and the girl Alsi, went around and about and in and out of dwellings and households, exhorting and talking, and pleading.

How many times did I enter a dark building, where a small glow of light lit up what seemed like a herd of beasts asleep on the floor. But they were our people, deep inside the animal pelts; and faces lifted unwillingly from under covering arms, or out of hoods of fur, and eyes watched me as I strode about, trying to impress on them that vigorous movement was indeed still possible. The eyes moved slowly, their gleam being extinguished at every moment as sleep closed them, then I saw them glitter again . . . it was like coming at dusk on a hillside where a herd of our great beasts had lain down to rest and, seeing us come near, they lifted their heads and stared, wondering if this time we were a danger, and then, deciding not, the shine of many pairs of eyes vanished as they turned away the great heavily horned heads. Oh, it was so stuffy and unpleasant in our dwellings now! How I disliked having to make my way into them, and stand there, trying to look alert and awake, when the foetid atmosphere, the general torpor, the cold, dulled my mind and made me want only to lie down with them all and sleep away my life—until Canopus came.

"Is Canopus here yet?"—I heard, everywhere, from these dark smelly interiors, and this anxious needy cry seemed to ring in my ears all the time as I went about my work.

We had managed to arouse enough young and strong people to extend the sheds and runs where Alsi was breeding the snow animals. These covered a large area near our town; and the system Alsi had worked out was in operation in all our towns. Being creatures of the cold, they did not need much shelter. We provided for them something like the caves which we believed were their original breeding places, made out of rock and piled with lichens and moss. The animals were kept in bounds by walls of the half-frozen earth of the tundra. They were now as important a source of food as the herds of great beasts. Feeding them was a problem we did not expect to solve. Vegetable matter of some sort was what they had to have, and their need for it competed with ours. They had learned to accept a diet of lichens, mosses, and the new kinds of low-growing tough plants that now were the planet's chief vegetation. But these were what we too were eating, made into broths and stews of all kinds, when we could not stand for one more minute the monotony of meat. But what these animals gave us was meat— again meat; but at least, because they seemed to thrive on so little, the return from them was greater than if we ate the lichens and the bitter woody plants.

To breed them was economic, was sensible. But we did not like them. Had no affection for them.

In captivity they had become clumsy, slow-moving animals, their whiteness dimmed by the necessary and inevitable dirt of their pens and caves. I often stood there beside Alsi, to watch them. She, this most capable and inventive tender of animals, did not like her work. She wore, often enough, a rueful sort of grimace on that pleasant broad face of hers; and her eyes that shone out of the deep hood of fur had an apology in them. For what? I knew, well enough! So did we all. When Alsi, or Klin, or Marl, or myself, had about us a certain look of deprecation, defensiveness, it was because we did not like what we had to do!

Imprisonment had changed, too, the nature of these creatures: they were unlikeable and unresponsive, and their bright expressionless blue eyes stared back at us from the soiled white faces. But in her own quarters, which she shared with brothers and a sister, Alsi had two of these little creatures as pets. And there they played and bounded about, and were delightfully affectionate. They greeted the approach of any one of us with little trills of pleasure, and they loved to nestle close or to creep into the folds of a coat or a scarf, where they lay blinking soft blue eyes that were all mischief and friendliness. Such was the real nature of the beasts we had made unpleasant prisoners.

Sometimes I went out by myself when there was soft snow falling, and stood quite still, and soon I saw a gentle darting movement which was not the blowing or settling of the snowflakes. If I stared long enough, my eyes attuned to what I hoped to see, this subtle shadowy movement took shape, and I was looking at the little snow animals, wild ones, that seemed to lift, and settle, and then run through the white fall, and then float up among the snow. Yes, I have seen that: how they ran and were airborne, sometimes for long distances, as if they were birds using air currents. And they alighted more softly than birds; and then a white plumy shape came into vision again quite high above the ground, at the level of my own gaze. For the flash of a moment blue alert friendly eyes shone into mine, and then there was a fast turning movement, like that of a water creature, and the white soft thing was floating away among the white blowing feathery particles. And I had met Alsi out there, doing the same: refreshing ourselves with this delightfulness, this soft delicious play in the snow—reminding ourselves of the real nature of the poor animals whom we had deprived. But what did they live on? There were few droppings from the great birds who lived on them, and these were usually covered over almost at once by fresh snowfalls. The lichens on the rocks and the plants had to be dug out by us from under snow. We came to believe, Alsi and I, that these creatures were nourished by snow; or, if we did not believe it, we enjoyed playing with the idea, making for ourselves a small place in our minds where fantasy and improbability could be enjoyed; and this was a resting place and a restorative for us, living as we did amidst a grinding necessity that narrowed us and pressed us down.

And then Canopus did come to us. Canopus came at last. It was Johor who came, but what I saw first was a tall figure in thick clothes standing not far from the pens and caves of our snow animals, looking into our town, with an alertness and interest that made me say at once, That is a stranger. For animation of any kind at all had to strike me as unusual. Then he turned his head towards me, and I saw his brown healthy face, already greying because of the crumbs of snow on his skin and his eyebrows, and I said: "Johor!" And he said: "Doeg!"

By then I was sleeping in a snow dome, or snow hut, thus relieving the pressure on space for others, but it was not a place I spent time in unless for sleep. Johor said: "Oh, it is cold! Where can we go?"

There was a long low shed near the animals' pens that Alsi used to store food and bedding for them, and I said: "In there . . ." And already I was feeling that my strong expectations for release were about to be killed dead, for there was nothing in his manner that signalled to me: Yes, now it is all over, your ordeal is over, and you are about to be set free. On the contrary, there was a stricture in his manner, a holding back, and an expression in his eyes that I recognised. For I saw it often enough, among ourselves, among us Representatives. He was feeling that pressure of patience that is born from watching others suffer, knowing that nothing one may say will alter the suffering, knowing that you yourself are a part of what they experience as pain. For of course we, the Representatives, making decisions, all of which had to be difficult and with oppressive results, were felt, by the people, as burdensome. It was we who said: "No, not yet." Who said: "Wait." Said: "Do not sleep in all day in your dark rooms, but rouse yourselves, work, do anything—no, bear the burden of your consciousness, your knowledge, do not lose it in sleep." Said: "So it is and thus it must be—at least, for a time." And this was nothing to do with us as individuals, for whoever they chose to represent them in this or that function, must say: "No." And: "This is all there is." And: "You must do without."

So what I saw in Johor's eyes was what I saw every day; and what I knew others saw in mine. I knew already that there were no fleets of rescue ships waiting somewhere just out of my line of sight on the tundra. I knew he had come to us alone.

I asked, knowing what he would say: "Your Space Traveller?"

He said gently: "I have sent it away. I shall be with you for—quite a little time."

I turned my face well away from him, knowing that he could not see it inside the deep fur, for I could not hide then what I felt.

We went into the shed. It was a long low place, with openings along one wall that led into the runs of the animals where food could be pushed in. Sacks of springy tough plants from the tundra were piled up and the smell from them was sharp and pleasant. I sat on one, enjoying the freshness, and Johor sat near. He brought out from his pockets some small red fruits, which I had not seen, and he held them out towards me on his palm. My hands went out to them as if I was going to grab and snatch, and, seeing my hands do this, I could not help shuddering at myself, and turning my face away. That gesture, which I could not help, said clearly enough what we all were now, what we had come to, and of course Johor had taken in its meaning.

Now he pushed back the hood from his head, and I saw him clearly. He had not changed. I enjoyed looking at the healthy gleam of the brown skin, the quick alertness of healthy eyes. I knew my eyes were feeding on the sight: I understood what those words meant, to feed on sight. And I pushed my head back and loosened my heavy coat, and his eyes took in what there was to be gathered from my face.

He nodded, and sighed.

I said: "If you have no fleet of Space Travellers, then there are no supplies of fresh food."

And he slightly shook his head.

"And yet we are not to be taken off from here at once?"

I knew I leaned forward to search his face, and he remained still, letting me look into his face and his eyes.

"We are not to be taken off," I said at last, and I heard my words ring out in the cold silence, and each word seemed to sink through the air, as if the air itself rejected them: the substance of my words was being refused by the air, and what I felt was this: If my words are true, then *what* is rejecting them?

"What has happened?" I said at last, and my voice was wild and angry.

He began to speak, and failed.

I said: "There is a paradise somewhere, we see it when we look up out of this sordid place, we see it shining in our cold skies, or rather we see its mother, a fruitful star. Rohanda will be our home,

Rohanda the generous one, Rohanda the planet where everything thrives, and where a race of people are being grown like particularly promising plants, grown by Canopus, to act one day as hosts for us, for the poor inhabitants of Planet 8, who also have been nurtured by Canopus, made and grown and fed by Canopus, so that they and we may come together in a match, and make of Rohanda a planet that Canopus itself will wonder over and admire. On that lovely planet wait for us even now warm oceans, and sunny fields and pleasant forests full of fruit and hillsides where grain is gold and white and rippling green as the soft winds move. On Rohanda there are storehouses full of the soft light clothes that will cover us and the fresh light food we will eat and everything, everything, everything we will look at will be coloured, we will live again among the colours of living things, we will see the infinite shades of green, and yellow and red—our eyes will again be fed with scarlet and gold and purple, and when we look up into the deeps of the skies our eyes will fill with blue, blue, blue, so that when we look into each other's eyes we will no longer see a crazed glare of white where colour has been bled out by whiteness, white, white, always white or grey or brown . . . yes, Canopus? Is that what you have come to tell us?"

"No," he said at last.

"Well then? How is Rohanda? Have you planned that another species, another of your genetic creations is to enjoy Rohanda?"

"Canopus keeps its word," he said, though his voice sounded strange enough.

"When it can?" I said.

"When it can."

"Well then?"

"Rohanda has . . . suffered the same fate as Planet 8, though not as terribly and suddenly."

"Rohanda is no longer lovely and fruitful?"

"Rohanda is . . . Shikasta, the broken one, the afflicted."

And now it began to come into me, what he was saying, my whole self was absorbing it, and I stilled my indignation, my wild rejection of what he was telling me. I sat there in my thick wad of hide, and I heard a keening cry come out of me—the same that had come from the populations when we stood around the lake, our sacred place, and knew we were going to destroy it.

I could not still this lament, not at once, not for wanting to, because I was thinking of the thousands of low dark dwellings everywhere on our little world where our people huddled like beasts, dreaming of sunny days and soft winds—dreaming of Rohanda and of their regeneration.

Johor did not move away, or spare me, or himself. He continued to sit there, quite close, his face open to my eyes.

And when I was at last quiet he said: "And Canopus *does* keep its word."

"When you can."

"In one way if not in another."

I knew perfectly well that the implications of this were too difficult for me to take in then. The words had that ring to them that words do when presenting to you for the first time truths with which you are going to have to become familiar—whether you want to or not! Oh yes, I was listening, and I knew it, to some new possibilities of growth being offered to me. Which I was going to have to aspire to . . . to grow towards . . . to *take in.*

But sorrowful indignation was still surging and sweeping in me, and I said to him: "On the other side of the planet, in Mandel, the great city, which we could emerge into if we could burrow straight through from here to there, is a civil war. They are killing each other. The dead are lying in heaps and mountains all around the city, because there is no way of burying them in the frozen soil, nor do we have any means of burning them for we have no fuel. The living—if you can call it living—go about what they have to do, surrounded by piles of their dead. And these are people who until such a short time ago did not have a word for murder. Or for war."

He sighed—and suffered. But did not turn his face away.

"How are we going to tell them, Johor?"

He said nothing.

"Are you going to tell them—you, Canopus? . . . No, for that is not your way. You will be with us for a little, and soon we, the

Representatives, will understand that everyone knows it already, but we will not know how this has happened."

And now I was silent a long while, for my mind seemed to want to open itself to something—I felt the pressure of some truth working there in its depths.

"Johor, what is it I have to understand?"

"Have you ever thought what being Representative is?"

"Do you imagine I have not lain awake at nights over it, have not thought, and wondered! Of course I have. That is what my life has been! Am I doing as I should for the best, making the good and proper decisions, working rightly and well with the other Representatives, expressing them as they . . ."

And my mind faded out again, into a place where truth was waiting for me.

"As they express me?" I asked at last.

"How did you become a Representative? When was it? Can you remember?"

"Funnily enough, it was only recently that I asked myself the same question. And it isn't easy to say exactly when it was. But I suppose you could say it was when several of us youngsters were assigned to work on a new section of the wall. We had to dig out the earth for the foundations. About twenty of us. Well, I became a spokesman for all of us."

"Yes, but how?"

"That is what is hard to say. I feel it was probably a series of chances. Any one of them could have become spokesman, and at different times all of them were."

"Any one of them could have represented the others?"

"Yes, I think so."

"And you were Masson, for that time?"

"No, not yet—Masson was instructing us. At that time Masson was very many, because of having to get the wall built. We youngsters were apprenticed to Masson. Klin and Marl were there too, but that was before they became Klin and Marl. We had our family names still. We were not born into the adult world, there was no pressure on us yet to choose our adult names. The next time I represented others was at harvest, but we were taking it in turns to speak for everyone, and to allot tasks. And so it went on. I did all kinds of work, just like all the others. And all of us at various times were Representatives."

"Yet some of these young people grew up to be Representatives and others did not?"

"Yes. I have been thinking about that. It is strange, for I can't see that those who did not were so different. And as for myself, I did not see myself then as someone who would be a Representative. I think it was not until I was Doeg that I became truly a Representative. Klin and Marl and myself were taken by Canopus to Planet 10. We were not formally instructed, but taken everywhere around it to see how their people lived, and how differently things were done there. It was the people from Planet 10 who were instructing the Rohandans, you say—before things went wrong there. But we did not know when we visited Planet 10 that there was any special link between us and those people, or could have been. But of course we could see that they were much more developed than we were. And when we three came back from Planet 10, we were all Doeg, for then we travelled everywhere over our planet and told what we had seen. And everyone marvelled—for before that people had not been taken abroad from our planet to other places. I wonder why you chose us, Johor? I remember wondering then! Because we were in no way different from any of the others. Perhaps we had all three done more of the different kinds of work than others, but not so very much more. No, when we talked about it, because of course we did among ourselves, we concluded that we were chosen because of our ordinariness. And we held on to that thought when we came back and became a nine days' wonder with our amazing stories. . . . It was then I first noticed that always when one is telling of something done or seen or experienced, it becomes a story, a tale . . . at any rate, our people listened as if to some tale or legend. But you have only to begin: We were taken to this or that city, and it was such a time of the day, and we were met by—and at once there is something marvellous about it, and they have to know what is going to happen next! And this is true even when you are telling of something quite ordinary, let alone of a new planet. Since then I have remained Doeg nearly all the time, though Klin and

Marl have not. Though I have been Klin and Marl and Pedug and Masson, when needed. But Doeg is my nature, I suppose."

"And when you were one of the five Representatives of the Representatives?"

"Oh, that was convenience, chance—people are chosen almost at random."

"Any one of the Representatives can represent the others?"

"Yes! You know that! You know everything I am telling you— yes, I understand that I have to tell myself what I know—but we sit here, we sit talking, you and I, the pair of us, and you prod and you push me to say things that I suppose are important . . ."

"Unless you expect me not to take you seriously when you ask questions? Shall I ignore them, because you already know the answers? Representative Doeg, whom do you represent? And what are you?"

He leaned forward at this, looking straight into my face, but what welled up in me then put an end to a moment that could have saved me so much questioning, and pain. But we may not hasten certain processes in ourselves: they have to work their way, and often enough, without our active or conscious aid.

I was thinking of our poor peoples; the pain of their fate invaded me, the waste of it, the waste . . .

Johor said drily: "This is a lavish and generous universe."

"You mean, it can afford the deaths of a few million people."

"Is death something new to you? Is it only now that you begin to contemplate death—what it means?"

"Are you saying to me that the deaths of old people who have had their lives and who have used them are the same as the deaths we have to confront now?"

"Have children and young people and even infants never died with you? Have you only had to come to terms with the deaths of the aged?"

"You cannot be saying to me that it does not matter if the populations of a whole planet have to die—a species?"

"I have not said it did not matter. Nor that we, Canopus, do not feel pain at what is happening. Nor, Doeg, that we have not done everything to prevent this happening. Nor that we are not . . ."

But indignation made me cut him short. "But you are not able to space-lift off this planet its doomed millions? You do not have a little unwanted planet somewhere that we could be given to use and develop and make fruitful? You have no use for us?"

"Are those really questions, Doeg? Very well, I shall treat them as such—though ask yourself, does Canopus, in your experience, deal in rhetoric? No, we are not able to take off from Planet 8 all your populations. We do not have the resources . . ."

But again I was so thoroughly possessed by indignation that I could not let him go on, and I exclaimed: "You do not have the resources! Or are you saying that *some* of us will be taken off, leaving the rest to their fates? If you are saying this, then I, for one, will refuse! I am not going to be saved at the expense of others! And I know that every one of the Representatives will say the same! We have not spent our lives working for our peoples, expressing our peoples, *being* our peoples, only to abandon them at the end. . . ." My mind blacked out there, and for a long time. I knew it had been a long time, when I came to myself and found I was sitting there, in the cold shed, opposite Johor, who was patiently waiting.

His eyes were keenly searching my eyes, my face.

What had gone on, inside me, during that long dark space, now made it impossible for me to challenge him as wildly and angrily as I had before. But after a time I heard myself bring out rather feebly: "It is strange, what you said then, that Canopus does not have resources for this or that . . . We have always thought of you as all-powerful, able to do what you like. We have never imagined you as limited. Limited by what, Johor?" And I answered myself: "You are the creation and creatures of something, some Being, to whom you stand in the same relation as we stand to you? . . . Yes, that must be so. But I have not thought on those lines before . . . And you cannot transcend your boundaries, as we may not transcend ours . . ." And here came welling up the rage again— "But Canopus has not suddenly found itself the subject of a cosmic accident! Your planet—or is it planets?—does your star nurture more than one dependent? Your planet has not found itself suddenly, and almost from one day to the next, blighted and cursed by some movement of stars so distant you probably have never even known they existed—have not even given names to?"

He said gently, humorously: "Well, not yet. But you know, it could happen to us, as it has happened to you."

"And to Rohanda."

"And to Rohanda." And here, at the name, he let out a sigh so deep and so painful that I had to cry out: "Ah, Johor, I wonder if you sigh and suffer for us, Planet 8, as I can see you do for Rohanda. Do you care for it so much? Is it so much more beautiful a place than this is—was? In talking to others, perhaps to your peers, on Canopus, do you sigh as you did then, at the word Rohanda, when someone says: Planet 8?"

He said: "It is true that I am at this time afflicted by Rohanda. I have just come from there. It is hard to see something as healthy and good and promising as Rohanda was lose it impetus, its direction."

"Worse than seeing us do the same?"

"You forget, the future of your planet was to be the future of Rohanda! We sent to Rohanda especially skilled and admirable colonists, from Planet 10, to make a synthesis with a species we were bringing to a certain level, so that you, from this planet, might make a synthesis with them, and become something quite extraordinary—so we hoped. . . ."

I said: "You were planning to take off our populations to Rohanda. You have resources and intention for *that*—but not to save us now."

"There is nowhere to take you. Our economy is a very finely tuned one. Our Empire isn't random, or made by the decisions of self-seeking rulers or by the unplanned developments of our technologies. No, we have a very long time ago grown out of that barbarism. Our growth, our existence, *what we are* is a unit, a unity, a whole— in a way that, as far as we know, does not exist anywhere else in our galaxy."

"So we are victims of your perfection!"

"Perfection is not a word we have ever used of ourselves—and not in thought either . . . that word belongs only—to something higher."

"Victims nevertheless."

I said this briskly, coldly, and with finality. I did not feel able to continue with the colloquy. I was tired in a way which had become only too familiar—as if every movement, every word, even a thought that came into my head—was too heavy and difficult. I needed to sleep.

"You can, if you need privacy, use my ice cave," I said. "But I have to sleep . . . I have to . . . I have to . . ."

As I sank down among my shaggy furs, I thrust towards him a skein of dried meats, and I saw him break off a piece and taste it, not with pleasure, but certainly with interest—Canopus was going to be *interested* in everything that happened, had to be, by its nature—even if this was the death of a planet. . . .

I woke to a consciousness of being awake: *I am here, in this heavy warmth of hides and furs.* I was understanding that while in happier days I had woken thus, thinking: *This is my condition, that was my sleep, I shall now move myself into this or that activity,* it had never been with this sharpness, this urgency.

The ease of our old sensuous life had not needed from us a certain kind of self-awareness. Now I came up through layers of sleep, and my body was supported on warmth as it might have been on the warm waters of our old life, and my mind was easy and free too, yet I knew that almost at once the strain and the pain of our new life must begin. I was wondering if this was how our vast shaggy beasts woke on a half-frozen hillside, muscles and bones relaxed inside their housing of shaggy pelt. Did they feel, as they lifted their heads, their eyes opening on a spin of snowflakes, that in a moment effort was going to drive through those cumbersome limbs of theirs, forcing them to their feet, and to the work of keeping themselves fed and fuelled . . . but meanwhile, while they lay there, they floated on sleep, and the good memories held in sleep . . . but up they must clamber, hooves slipping on rocks and pebbles, and their teeth would scrape on the surfaces of bitterly cold stones for the lichens there, and soft noses would be pushing aside loose snow to reach the earth that is half vegetable, the earth food that lies thick and uncomfortably on the stomach? I was beast with them, inside beast's covering, thinking of beast's food, and so strong was my identification with them that I felt cold air sinking in through the mats of hair on my shoulder and half believed it wind, and I turned my head and saw Johor come quietly in a door he opened as little as he could, shutting it at once against the cold.

He sat down on a heap of half-dried heather, and looked at me. I quickly shut my eyes, for I did not feel, yet, like facing the effort of making my mind meet his.

"There is a blizzard," he said—for he knew I was awake. "No one is out—I have been from house to house through the town and in each one, they are lying as you do, silent and still inside layers of hides."

I was looking up at the roof over us: a mass of heather over which had been piled sods and earth. There was a bloom of frost on the heather, and on the stone of the walls.

"And as you stood there in the doorways," I said, "you saw heads lift, one after another, and the eyes shine up at you, and then go out, as the heads were lowered back into sleep."

"Yes. Back into sleep."

"Back into the dark from which we all come."

"Back into the—light from which we all come."

"I have not been dreaming of the light, Johor! I came to myself out of . . ."

"What?"

"Something sweet and wonderful—I know that. Something I long for."

"The light. A world of dazzling light, all a shimmering marvel—where the colours you yearn to see are shining—from whence you came."

"So you say, Johor."

"And where you will return."

"Ah, but when, when, *when* . . ."

"When you earn it, Doeg," he said, softly, but strongly enough to make me move inside my skins, stretch, and take on the burden of my limbs that did not want to feel my weight—the weight of living. The weight of thought. . . .

But I made myself sit up and face him.

"And they," I said, "those poor people huddled there dreaming of paradises that were falsely promised to them—how will they earn it? How will they reach the light at last—wherever it might be, for you haven't told me that, Johor."

He looked hard at me and said: "Representative Doeg, when you lie there dreaming, do you imagine your dreams are only yours—do you imagine that you spin dreams out of yourself that are uniquely yours? Do you believe that when you come to yourself from a world of dreams you think no one else shares, your consciousness of yourself, this feeling *I am here, Doeg is here*—belongs only to yourself, and no one else shares that feeling? As you come awake, feeling *This is Doeg, this is the feeling of me, Doeg*—how many others are at the very moment coming awake all over your planet, thinking *This is me, this is the feeling of me?*"

It was bitter to me, to let go that little place I was able to rest on, take refuge in—the thought, *This is me, I, Doeg*—and I resisted.

I said: "Not long ago I was a quick-moving, slender, brown-skinned creature, who woke in the morning thinking: Soon I will step out into a sun that will polish my brown skin into little gleams of colour, and the air will flow in and out of my lungs in balmy mildness . . . that was I, then, that was Doeg. And now I am a thick heavy greasy creature with dull greyish brown skin. But I am still Doeg, Johor—that feeling has stayed—and so, now, you say I must let that go too. Very well, I am not the elegant handsome animal I was, and I am not this lump of uncouthness. But I still come up out of sleep and feel: *Here I am. I recognise myself. It is I who lie here, after so many journeys and adventures in my sleep.*"

"Your shared sleep."

"My shared waking—very well then, Johor, what am I to hold on to in this—blizzard that is blowing away everything, everything, everything . . ."

"Do you remember how we, Canopus, came to you all and gave you instruction in what made you, made your world?"

"Yes, it was not long before you came to us and told us to build—the wall that would shield us from the ice."

"Which has, and does shield you from the ice."

"Which would have done better to give way long ago, putting an end to this long dreariness and torment."

"No."

"Because there is something left to be done? What? You have come all the way here from your place in the galaxy, and you have sent away your Traveller, and you sit here with me in this shed, and . . ."

"Well, Representative?"

"What do I represent, Johor?"

"Do you remember what we taught you?"

I sat up in my nest, and pulled up the thick coverings all around me and over my head, so that only my face was bare. Close to me, Johor's face showed under his hood.

"I remember how we first understood that you were teaching us something in a way none of us had done before—directly. You asked us all to go up into the hills on the other side of the wall, and to choose a place where the ground rose all around. We massed there, all of us from the town and from a long way about. You asked us to bring one of the animals—those that are extinct now— that we intended to kill for food. You asked us to have it killed before the people assembled, and we, the Representatives, were pleased that the act of killing was not to be associated with your presence, for while we did not conceal what lay behind our eating of meat, we tried to see that there was no reason to dwell on it all—the slaughterhouses, the preparations. For when we came to- gether to discuss this particular thing, we Representatives, we always found for some reason a reluctance in us, a fear, to do with this business of killing other animals. It has always seemed to us that here was an area of danger. Something that could take hold and spread—and yet we did not remember Canopus ever saying any- thing about it."

"One of four species that were used to make you was easily roused to killing. Some of us on Canopus did not wish to make use of that material, but others did, for this was—and still is—a physi- cally strong species, enduring, able to bear hardship."

"When we all stood there on those hillsides looking down at that dead antelope, and my old friend Marl took up the knife to cut it open, I felt thrills of sensation all through me—and I was afraid to call this pleasure, but I knew that it was. And when the stomach was split from throat to tail, and the guts fell out, I knew how easy it would be to plunge my hands into that mass and then . . ." A red mist blew across my mind, and when it had gone, the frosty twigs of the roof, the grey rocks, the pinched face of Johor looked even more meagre and ugly.

"Yes," he said, "you did well to be careful."

"Yet you called us there, to watch the body of that animal cut up. We stood under a warm sun, and the wind brought us the spicy scents from the lake, and we saw the guts laid in a heap there, with the heart and the liver and the other organs, the head and the tail and the hide together, and the bones laid bare like the branches of a tree. And we were restless and moved about on our hillsides, and we sniffed at the scent of blood which seemed to belong to our memories, and then you came out from among us and stood surrounded by those bloody bits of meat and bone. And you said to us, 'You are wondering, every one of you, where the beast has gone—where what is real of the beast, as you know it. Where its charm, its friendliness, its grace, its way of moving that delights you. All of you know that what is lying here is not what is true about this dead beast. When we look around at the hillsides, where the wind is rippling the grasses and whitening the bushes, we see there the same spirit that was the truth of this dead animal—we see a quickness and freshness and delight. And when we look up now at the play of the clouds—there is the reality of the beast. And when we look around at each other and see how beautiful we are, again we see the beast, the pleasantness and rightness of it . . .' And so you spoke, Johor, for a long time, before you stopped talking of beauty and grace. Then you bent over the piles of meat and bones, and you held up in your bare hands the heart, and you said to us that each one of us is a package of hearts, livers, kidneys, entrails, bones, and each one of these is a whole and knows itself. A heart knows it is a heart and feels itself to be that. And so with a liver and every other thing inside every animal, inside you. You are a parcel, a package of smaller items, wholes, entities, each one feeling its identity, saying to itself, Here I am!—just as you do, in moments of sensing what you are. But this assembly of heart, lungs, skin, blood, packaged so tight and neat inside a skin, is a whole, is a creature. . . . And you made us laugh, Johor, standing there on that lovely morning, which I remember as colour, colour—blues and greens and soft reds and yellows—saying that a liver probably believed it was the best and highest organ in a body, and a heart too, and the blood too, and perhaps they even believe that a body is made up entirely of heart, or liver or blood. . . . Yes, I remember how we all laughed. And that was how that lesson ended. And when Canopus came again to visit us, you brought with you the instruments for seeing the very small, and for a long time, every one of us, down to the smallest child, studied the very small through these instruments."

"And what did you remember of that occasion, what stayed with you most strongly? Was it the unlikeable sight of the bloody organs spilled out on the ground, and your pity for the beast?"

"No, it was how you taught us to look for the charm and quickness of the animal everywhere—in the movement of water, or the patterns flocks of birds used to make as they swirled and darted and flowed about the sky."

Alsi came sliding quickly into the shed, opening the door as little as she could. She was heavy and clumsy in her carapace of skins. She smiled at the two of us, though, and went about her work of pushing the heathers and lichens and bark through the openings into the pens of the snow animals. It took a long time, and I was remembering how quick she had once been. When she had finished she stood in front of us and opened the front of her coat, and we saw there the little confiding face of one of her pets, with its bright blue eyes, and she stroked it, in a way that said how she needed this contact with aliveness, with trust, and she said: "The Representatives for the Lake say that there are few creatures left in it."

"Do not worry," I said, as Johor did not speak. "We shall not be needing much more food."

She nodded, for she was already beginning to understand what was happening. She said: "News comes in from many towns and villages now that the people have decided not to eat, but to let themselves die."

Johor said: "Please collect together as many of you as have the will for it, and go to these places and say to them, Canopus asks you to stay alive for as long as you can. Say it is necessary."

"It is necessary?"

"Yes."

"Although we shall all die very soon?"

This was only the breath of a reproach, and she found it hard to look at him. But she did, and there was such a bewilderment there he felt it strike him—I could see how he shifted his limbs about inside the skins, as if he were adjusting himself to take on a physical burden. She was such an honest direct creature, so strong, so fine—and she had not let herself go at all into the general lassitude and indifference.

"There is more than one way of dying," he said gently.

He looked straight into her eyes. She looked back. It was a moment when invisible doors seemed to want to open, want to let in truths, new knowledge. . . . I could feel in myself these pressures. I was watching her eyes, so bravely searching Johor's. Meanwhile she stroked and stroked the head of her little friend, who looked up at her with such trust.

"Very well," she said. "I will see that the message gets to them all."

And Johor nodded, in a way that said: Yes, I can count on you, and she slid out again, letting in the roar of the storm outside, and a flurry of white flakes that did not melt, but lay in a patch on the stone of the floor near the door.

I said to Johor: "It is easier to bear the news of the death of a million people than to think that Alsi will die of starvation inside a heap of stinking furs. And I hate that in me, Johor. I have never been able to accept that partiality in us."

"You are complaining that we constructed you inadequately," he remarked, not without humour.

"Yes, I suppose I am. I cannot help it. I have never been able to see someone weep and agonise because of the death of someone close, yet respond not at all to some general ill or danger, without feeling I am in the presence of some terrible lack, some deep failure."

"You forget that we did not expect for you such ordeals."

"Ah, Canopus, you do indeed expect a lot of us poor creatures, who are simply not up to what is needed!"

"And yet when Alsi stood there just now, and took on so well and so bravely what I asked her, it seemed to me that as a species you are proving to be very capable of what is needed."

"Again, one person, one individual is made to represent so many!"

And, as I spoke, I felt the now familiar pressures, the announcement deep in myself of something I should be understanding.

And that was when I let myself go away into sleep, having taken in what I could for that time. And when I woke Johor was sitting patiently, waiting for me to resume. I had not done much more than register: Here I am!—and add to it the thought: But the "I" of me is not my own, cannot be, must be a general and shared consciousness—when Johor said: "Doeg, tell me what you all learned during that long time when you studied the material of your planet through the new instruments."

It was very quiet. The raging of the wind had stopped. I imagined how outside the snow would be lying in billows of fresh white. Through the snow Alsi would be pushing her way, waist high, accompanied by those she had been able to rouse, and others would be trudging to the near towns and villages wondering if they would get there before the storm came again and crowded the air with white, white, white . . .

"We learned that everything is made up of smaller things. And these of the smaller and finer . . . these organs of ours, a heart or a liver, which we don't think of at all, but know are there, doing their work, are composed of all sorts of parts, of every kind of shape—strings and lumps and strips and layers and sponges. And these bits and pieces are made up of cells of all kinds. And these— every one of which has an energetic and satisfactory life of its own, and a death too, for you can observe these deaths, like ours—are composed of clusters of smaller living units, and molecules, and then these are made up again of just so many units, and these too . . ."

My eyes, which had in fancy been dissecting a lump of flesh, a heart, seeing it dissolve into a seethe of tiny life, now again perceived Johor, a mound of skins, from which a pallid face showed. But even so, it was unmistakably Johor who sat there, a presence, a strength—a *solidity*.

"Johor," I said, "I sit here feeling myself solid, a weight of matter, dense, with a shape I know every slope and surface of, and my mind is telling me that this is nothing—for I know that through what we have seen with your devices."

"What then was there when you came to the minutest item that we can see?"

"There is a core—of something. Yet that dissolves and dissolves again. And around it some sort of dance of—pulsations? But the spaces between this—core, and the oscillations are so vast, so vast . . . that I know this solidity I feel is nothing. A shape of mist, I am, a smear of tinted light, as when we see—or *saw*, for we see only snow now, filling the spaces of sunlight—a spread of light with motes floating there. I am, from a perspective of vision very far from my own proper eyes, not dense or solid at all . . . But Johor, while I can see what it is you have been leading me to say to you, that this heaviness . . . for I am so heavy, so heavy, so thick and so heavy I can hardly bear it—this heaviness is nothing at all. A shape of light that has in it particles slightly denser in some places than in others. But what my mind knows is of no use to my lumpishness, Johor. What you see of me, with those eyes of yours that belong to another planet, a differently weighted star—I can imagine, for I have seen cells and molecules disappear into a kind of dance, but . . ."

"A dance that you modify by how you observe it. Or think of it," he remarked.

The silence that is a listening deepened around us. But the claims of my discomfort and my impatience made me break it. "And yet this nothingness, this weight and labour of matter that lies so painfully on us all, is what you work with, Johor, for you sit here, you sit in this freezing place, and what you say is, Don't let yourselves die yet, make the effort to keep alive—and what you are wanting to keep alive are these bodies, the flesh that disappears when you look at it with different eyes, into a something like motes with the sun on them."

Yes, I did sleep then, dropped off, went away, and came back remarking: "I have often wondered, when I looked at the tiny oscillations and pulsations that compose us, where, then, are our thoughts, Johor? Where, what we feel? For it is not possible that these are not matter, just as we are. In a universe that is all gradations of matter, from gross to fine to finer, so that we end up with everything we are composed of in a lattice, a grid, a mesh, a mist, where particles or movements so small we cannot observe them are held in a strict and accurate web, that is nevertheless nonexistent to the eyes we use for ordinary living—in this system of fine and finer, where then is the substance of a thought?

"I watch myself, Johor . . . I feel myself . . . inside this mass of liquids and tissues and bones and air which is so heavy, so very heavy, but which is nevertheless nothing, scarcely exists—when I feel anger, does anger blow through the interstices of the mesh and web which is what I know myself to be? Or when I feel pain, or love . . . or . . . I say these words, and everyone knows what I mean by anger, by wanting, by loss, and all the rest, but do you have instruments on Canopus that can see them? Can you see them, Johor, with those different eyes of yours? Do you see me sitting here, this poor beast Doeg, as a smear of tinted light, changing in colour as rage or fear sweeps through me? Where from, Johor? The substance of our flesh, the matter which makes us, dissolves into—vast spaces, defined by the movements of a dance. But we have not yet put fear or loneliness under instruments."

I went off to sleep again—into a dream so vivid and satisfying and detailed that it was a world as strongly defined as anything I had known in waking life, on our planet or on any other. The landscape I moved through had something of our planet about it, and yet was not; events, people, feelings—all were known to me, yet not in ordinary life. And I had dreamed this dream before, and recognised it, or rather, the setting of the dream. As I entered the dream I was saying to myself, Yes, I know this place, because *I know its flavour*. And I woke after some sort of interval, long or short, and the atmosphere of the dream was so strong that I brought it with me, and it lay shimmering, in beguiling colours that were the stuff of memory to us now since colour had been taken from our world, over the frosty greys and browns of the inside of the shed. And then the dream faded, and I said: "I have been dreaming."

"Yes, I know. You have been laughing and smiling, and I have been watching you."

"Johor, I could tell you the story of my dream, for it had a structure, a beginning and a development and an end, just like the tales of Doeg, the storyteller, and I could describe the incidents and the adventures and the people in it, some of them I know and some unknown—but I could never describe the *atmosphere* of the dream, although it is an atmosphere so strong, and unique to this dream, and to this cycle of dreams, that I could never mistake it. From the first moment I enter this particular landscape of dream, or even as I approach it from another dream, I know it, I know the air, the feel, the taste of it. I could not describe to you or to anyone what this atmosphere is. There are no words for it. And yet the realms of emotions and of thoughts are analogous to those of dreams. For an emotion has a flavour and a taste, a *feel* to it, that is not describable in words, but you can say to anyone 'love' or 'longing' or 'envy'—and they will know exactly what you mean. And the emotions in you that are of the class of 'love' will have the same quality, and will be the same to everyone else, so the word 'love' is a communication, we know what we mean. And when a thought, which is properly colourless and tasteless, is tinged with grief, or vindictiveness, it has a taste, its own being, so, experiencing this grief-laden or joy-bringing thought, first there is the experience and then the word and I say to you, or to Alsi, 'I am thinking a thought that has the quality of joy,' and you and everyone shares my experience. And this flavour or taste *is a substance*, is matter, is material, for everything is, everything must be; for if the minute dance that dissolves at the core which is no core at the heart of an atom is material, then so must be passion or need or delight. Can you, Johor, see where the pulses of the atom dissolve into patterns of movement of which you can say: This is envy, this is love?

"How does the material or substance of love modify that minuscule dance? How relate? For it is the *physical* substance of our bodies, our hearts, that breeds love or hate, or fear or hope—is that not so?—and cannot be separate from it. The wind that is love must arise somewhere in those appalling spaces between the nub of an atom and its electrons that dissolve, like everything else, into smaller and smaller, and become a fluid or a movement—or a *door into somewhere else?*

"I can ask you this question, knowing I share this with you, saying *love*, saying *fear*—and then I come back to the realm of dreaming, in which I spend a third of my life, which is soaked through and through with emotions, but also with sensations and feelings that have nothing to do with emotions, but are more to be described or suggested as colours suffusing a thing or a place—I can say, 'Johor, I have been dreaming,' coming back to this world here, and my dreams will have been more vivid than my waking, and the atmosphere I have spent my sleep-journeyings in will be one I have known all my life, since babyhood, and *I cannot find a word* that will convey this feel, or taste, or colour, or sensation to you or to anyone else. This is the ultimate solitude, Johor . . . and yet I wonder, when you say, 'I have been watching you sleep—watching you dream—' if you, with those eyes of yours that are made in the planet of a star weighted differently than ours, can say as you watch: 'Doeg is moving in *that* landscape of sleep, that place, meeting these and these people—Doeg is *partaking of the substance of that place* —I know he is, because I can see the substance of that other place, or time, or pulse, moving in the spaces of the subatomic particles, or movements' . . . and if this is so, Johor, then it lifts a little of the loneliness of knowing that there is nothing I can say, even to my closest friends, that will convey to them the flavour of a dream."

"When you dream, do you imagine you dream for yourself alone, Doeg? Do you think that when you enter a realm in your sleep it is familiar only to you? That you alone of the peoples of this little planet of yours know that particular realm? You may not be able to find a word to describe it so that others may know where you have been, but others know it, because they too move there as they dream."

And that is where that colloquy ended, because Alsi came in, with Marl and with Masson, and Zdanye, and with Bratch and with Pedug who had had the care of the Education of the Young before The Ice.

While Johor and I had sat there in that cold shed, waking and dreaming, around the pole that still was free of the snow and the ice, had come the slight movement towards warmth that we now called summer. In a space it would have taken us twenty of our days to walk across was an area of growth, and for the first time a kind of plant we did not know. It was very quick-growing, springing up into its full height in a few days, a frail sappy bush, aromatic, laden with blue flowers—and it covered the whole of this part of our globe, perhaps an eighth or a tenth of it. Klin, who usually worked down there through the year, had been visiting a valley nearer to the middle of the planet, which had been very warm and productive, hoping that it still might be mild enough to grow something, even if only heathers and brackens. But it was not; it was filled with snow, and so he had left it to go back to the polar regions, and had been met by messengers saying that herds of our great beasts were converging from everywhere to reach fields and hillsides covered with a new plant, which filled the air with scents new to us all. And by the time Klin reached ten days' walking distance from the pole, where tundra and greyness met this brief summer land, he saw that these herds, multitudes of them, covered everything, trampling and rearing and lowing, and making the earth shake with their delight, their intoxication at this marvel—fresh sappy aromatic food. They were drunk with it all, were lumbering around, and tossing up their enormous heads as if the weight of horns there was nothing, and roaring and even prancing, and it broke the heart, said Klin, to see these desperate hungry beasts released there, into a happiness and lightness—if one could call these heavy chargings and buttings light—yet, if you had become used to seeing a landscape filled with heavy melancholy animals, heads drooping, sniffing at the earth fodder with dislike, yet eating it; animals that seemed hardly able to move, and that slid and slipped and fell on icy places when they did move—if this was how, with pain and compassion, you had become used to seeing them—then, by contrast, this sudden energy was a wonderful thing.

But it was not only the herds that longed for freshness and greenness: they were eating, were consuming, what might be useful to our populations. From the towns and villages near the polar regions, people were roused up with promises of new fresh food, and they came blinking and stumbling out from their smelly dark places into the familiar greyness—but saw beyond the thick low snow clouds a pale blue, our frail fleeting summer. And, as they came down towards the pole through bitter tough stems and sprigs of the plants of the tundra, they saw in front of them blue, a blue haze spread over the earth, as if the skies had fallen, or as if the earth had taken to reflecting the skies. And even the weight of the great beasts, crowding and massing everywhere, could not completely hide the loveliness of these blue-flowered plants. And the air was full of a spicy tangy scent, which revived the people, banished their terrible indifference and lethargy. They divided into bands, and drove the beasts off half of the fertile lands—for we did not want to deprive them altogether, we needed their meat, and had been afraid that they too would be extinct soon, so little was there for them to eat. The plants sprang up again at once where the beasts had grazed them to the earth—sheets of pale blue lay everywhere. And the people, flinging off their coats of thick hides, lay among these flowering bushes, weeping with joy, and even rolling, or running about and jumping, as the poor beasts had done—but were not doing now, in their more confined and restricted space, but were eating steadily, and as quickly as they could, filling themselves while they could, for they seemed to know that this bounty would not be permanent—it was already halfway through this "summer" of ours, which no longer grew fruit, or grains, or vegetables, and had recently been growing very little more than sparse grasses. Yet here was this miracle, this marvel, that you could walk for twenty days through green and blue, under blue skies where the clouds of our old world—white and thick and lazy and delightful—moved all day, as if they knew nothing of the dark sullen cloud masses that crammed the horizons.

After a day on these aromatic pastures, our people were reborn, were their old selves: it was clear that the plants held some vital and powerful principle for health. Klin sent messages to Bratch, who was the Representative for Health, and he came, and sent for his helpers, and soon this plant, which grew again as quickly as it was cut, had made quantities of a kind of hay, that was more dried flowers than foliage, and then—it was a question of deciding how to apportion the life-giving food, for there was not enough of it to provide our people with even a mouthful each.

Who was to be benefitted? On what basis was it to be decided?

Klin and Marl and Masson and Pedug and Bratch, standing around inside the shed, telling us all this, were restless; wanted, we could see, not to be there, had in their minds the sight of the fair brief world of the polar summer which they had reluctantly left to confer with me, with other Representatives in the area—and with Johor. But I could see they scarcely looked at him, their eyes seemed to move over and away from him. And this was not only because they had not before seen him so clearly as a being like ourselves, suffering and pallid inside a caul of beasts' skin, but because they did not expect anything from him. Yet no one had said to them: "This planet will not be saved, the promises made to us are without a future." Before, it was to have been expected that everyone would come up to Johor, saying: "Canopus, where are your fleets of Space Travellers, when will you take us all away?" But no one said this. And Johor stayed quietly sitting on a heap of sacks filled with furze.

"Why stay here, in this dying place," said Marl, "even for as long as we need to confer—come, we will go down to the summer, and we can make our decisions there."

And so we, Johor and I, and all of them, and ten of the other Representatives, pushed our way through the snows around our town, and then stumbled and slid down hillsides, and mountain passes where we believed we would die of the cold, and down again to where ahead of us we could see blue, only blue—blue skies and blue earth—and a keen wind brought to us not the sharpness of cold but warm balmy smells that we had forgotten. And my eyes seemed to be swelling and growing, as they fed on the colours for which they were starved. . . . And yet, even as I stumbled towards the blue and lovely summer ahead, I was saying to myself, I, a smear or haze of particles on which light shines, I, a nothing, a conglomerate of vast spaces defined by a dance my mind cannot comprehend, am running forward into—nothing, for if I saw this summer land as Johor does, with his Canopus eyes, I would see a universe of space in which faint shapes drift and form and dissolve—I, nothing, run forward towards nothing, weeping as I run—and where live the emotions that make these tears, Johor? Where in the great spaces in the faint mist that I am, where in the fluid flowing structure of the dance of atoms, where . . . and how . . . and what, Johor?

When we reached the hillsides where green showed under the bushes laden with blue flowers, we flung ourselves down and rolled and, seated above the summer with the snow peaks and half-frozen lands at our backs, looking into a sunlight where drifted cloud shadows and sudden chills and reminders of the winter that would soon come down again over this scented miracle, we talked about what we must do, what we had to do.

We talked. Johor did not, though he sat among us as if he was one of the conferring group.

Our problem was practical: when we had decided who was to benefit from this food, how was it to be conveyed? Movement between villages and towns had ceased, except for teams who dragged in the supplies of dried meat. How were we to carry loads of this light but bulky stuff up into the snow and the ice, and, when it was distributed, were they to cook and eat it, or eat it as it was— for all of us were eating the flowers straight off the bushes without ill-effects, apart from the mild stomach disorders which we had to put up with as an aspect of what we had to expect now. At last Bratch suggested that we should pile the dried plant into the ponds and the water holes, hoping that the enlivening principle in it would be transferred to the water. Some of the water could be carried in containers up into the snow-covered lands, but soon the bogs and marshes would freeze again as the cold came back and we could send down teams with sledges to transport this ice, or even to drag up chunks of it across the snow. And, meanwhile, send messengers everywhere to say that this shallow summer was here, providing vegetable matter for those who could or would make the effort to come and enjoy it.

Some of those who were making the living fence to keep the

herds off the part of the harvest we had allocated for the use of our peoples went off to make sure the news reached all the populated centres. As for us, we stayed where we were, using every hour of daylight to pile the hay into the bogs and fens. The weather was not hot enough to make fermentation an immediate problem. The earth-smelling waters of these moorlands soon were emitting the fragrance of the plant, and our nights were spent lying out among the living plants, mostly awake, for we knew that this time of reprieve would soon end. The stars shone down, but not with the hard cold brilliance in blackness of the nights of the expedition up to the other pole: this was a distant mild shining, and they were continually going out as mists and veils blew across our skies.

By the time the messengers had come back, the plants had ceased to spring up again as they were cut; shadow lay more often on the hills and valleys than sun did; and the winds were not balmy, but made us shelter inside our deep coats. And the herds were no longer rearing and charging about, or bellowing, but were silent again. We all of us went to a place where we could look down on a valley crammed with these beasts, who stood with lowered heads above earth where there was no longer any green, or blue, or the soft blowing movement of growing things. We looked at a bull standing close to us, with the group of females that he served, and the calves of that season—there had been very few calves born for many seasons. We saw in the disconsolate, discouraged set of his shoulders that he felt himself a failure—lacking—hurt; for once again he would be commanding a group perpetually hungry, not able to breed, since nature was saying no, there is no future; once again they would have to lower their soft muzzles to the dense earth that is half-vegetable, forcing the unliked stuff into their stomachs that only partially digested it. And the females were anxious to keep their calves near them, and their eyes were red and wild, and they licked and maintained these small replicas of themselves with a desperation that said everything of the emotions that filled them. From horizon to horizon, the herds stood there—waiting. And we, too, now would have to return to our waiting.

There were about forty of us Representatives on that slope above the herds, and a hundred or so of those who had taken the messages to the people. Some people were coming in, in small groups, to take their share of the harvest, which was so sparse now, and they too rolled around in the green and ate the flowers. But only a few had been able to rouse themselves from their torpor and make the journey. We stood, a small multitude, in a hollow between low hills.

Long before those times of The Ice, I had learned to watch the disposition of people, events, what is said and what is not said—so as to understand what was likely to happen—*what was already happening, but not yet fully disclosed.* Those crowds standing about there, again huddling into the thick skins, watching the skies where the first snow clouds were massing, were not differentiated in any way, and Johor stood among them, almost unnoticed, though everyone knew that Canopus was among us. Soon we Representatives moved out of the mass of people and up on to a slope. It was because this was expected of us; we could see, feel, sense, that we should do this. But Johor stayed where he was.

And when we stood there, the forty of us, looking at the mass of people, and they stood looking at us, there was a long silence. What was happening?—we all wondered that, for usually the verbal exchanges between the two, represented and Representatives, were brisk enough: practical. Usually it was evident what had to be done by everyone. We had never had to make speeches, or exhort, or persuade, or demand—as I have seen done on other planets, and read about. No, there had always been a consensus, an understanding among us all, and this had meant that it had been a question of: so-and-so will see to this, and such and such will be done—by someone. And it was at these times that a Representative who felt a change was needed would step back into the mass, or someone who felt entitled and equipped would step up into the Representative group. But long silences had not been our style at all. We were looking closely at each other, examining each other: we them, and they, closely and carefully, us. We stood there a very long time. On one side the herds stretched away to the horizon, where the storms were raging black on white. On the other, trampled and fading meadows sent up the faintest reminiscent breath of the now past summer. Over us the skies were grey and low, and a few snowflakes spun down, and melted at once on faces, on our still exposed hands. And we searched each other's faces, as if examining our own: *What was happening?* Well, I know now, but then I did not. I did feel as if I were being elected, but in a capacity previously not experienced. I felt tested, probed, almost handled by those eyes that were so thoughtfully focussed on me and the rest of us Representatives. And, looking at them, it was as if I had not seen them before, not properly, not as I was seeing them now. So close we all were to each other, in this desperate and terrible enterprise that would involve us all, and in ways we could only partly know.

And while this long exchange went on, this silence that needed no words at all, Canopus stood there, part of the mass, quite passive and quiet. Yet nearly everyone in that throng, except for Alsi and—I think—Klin, still talked as if they believed Canopus would take us all off and away. That was still what we *officially* expected; and how—sometimes, but increasingly less frequently—we spoke. But not one of those people that day said to Johor: Canopus, where are your fleets that will take us all away from here, when will you keep your promise to us?

No, and it was not that there was reproach in the air, or anger, or accusation or even grief. That was the remarkable thing: the sober, quiet, responsible feeling among us, that did not admit grief, or mourning, or despair. Far away, deep in the snow-filled lands, where our friends lay in dark holes piled with hides, was the lethargy of grief, of despair. But here, among these few who had made the effort to travel to where the summer was, there was a different feeling altogether. And, after a long time, while we all stood there, *looking* at each other, it came to an end: we seemed to decide all at once, by some inner process, that it was enough. And everyone went off to the bogs and ponds, to see if they were frozen yet. No, but there was a thickening of the water's surfaces, and a breeze rippling them made wrinklings, then flakes and then cakes of the thinnest ice; and when we all roused ourselves next morning, where we lay together on the slopes above the water, we saw that the water had frozen over, was white, though with the blackness of bog water under it, and in the water the green and blue plant masses. We had to send out a party to drive off some young beasts from the herds, and kill them, and prepare food, since the harvest was over and no hay remained, nor fresh plants. The smell of blood came on the cold wind to us, and we heard the beasts nearest to us bellow and moan, as they, too, smelled the blood. And we wearily began again on this diet of ours, of meat, and meat, and meat, from which we had enjoyed so brief a respite.

In a few days the waters were solid ice, and we cut out great chunks, and piled these on to sledges, or tied ropes around them, and everywhere could be seen long lines of us bent over the toil and labour of transporting the ice blocks—white against white, for everywhere it was white again, snow covering all the earth, snow-heavy clouds above us, the snowy mountain peaks ahead. And the wind spun the snow off the drifts to meet the white eddies from the skies.

Heading in every direction went the plodding lines of white figures, and our team climbed straight up through the frozen passes and into the middle areas of our planet where, far ahead, we could see rearing up into a grey sky the white mass of our wall which, as we neared it, seemed like a vast water wave that had frozen in the moment before it fell. The jagged fanged crest stretched from horizon to horizon, overtopping a wall which was white now, all iced over, and with snow packed to half its height.

When we approached our own town, with our sledges piled with the ice we had brought with us, people went ahead to rouse up the sleepers. But again, only a few came staggering out, groaning and complaining, hardly able to see because of the glare after their long sojourn in half-dark. We pressed them: Try this ice we have brought—suck it, take it inside and melt it down, drink the water, see if you, too, will become invigorated and refreshed. And some did, and were enlivened, and did not return to their terrible death-in-sleep. For many were dying as they slept, and could not be revived, not with all the skills of Bratch.

About a quarter of the population of our town stood in the deep snow of the central square, and Klin and Marl and Alsi and Masson and Pedug and Bratch were there, and I, and Johor. And again there was the long silence, which went on for as long as it was necessary for—*what?* But it was not broken at all, but seemed to confirm and to feed us all. And, when this process had gone on, and on, something happened that was different from the other silence down on the slopes on the polar land. Johor stepped out a little way from the crowd, and stood there, quite still, looking at us all. It was as if he were *giving us an opportunity for something . . . for what?* His eyes went from face to face, and we could see how wan and worn he was, as unhealthy as the rest of us, in spite of our little excursion into summer.

Oh, it was so dark there, so dark, with the storms driving all around us, the thick low clouds above, the sombre ice wall rearing up behind us, and the darkness was an expression of what I was feeling then, for on Johor's face, which was humble in his patience in enduring, there was a look that said he had hoped for something from us all that was not yet there . . . he could see in the faces now turned towards him what he had stepped out by himself to evoke, but had hoped not to evoke. They were crowding around him, and saying: "Johor, are the space-fleets coming? When? How long must we wait?"—Yet these things were being said in voices quite at odds with the questions: as if a part of the questioners was asking, a part that even the questioners themselves were half-aware of or not aware of at all—suddenly everyone seemed to me to be asleep or even drugged or hypnotised, for these muttering questions were like those coming out of sleep. Yes, it seemed to me as I stood there, slightly to one side, as Johor was, looking at the faces, that I was among sleepwalkers who did not know what they were saying, and would not remember when they woke. And I was wondering if these queries had always sounded so to Johor: "Where are your space-fleets, Canopus, when will you save us?" And I wondered more than that, in the sharp moment of clarity, when everyone around me seemed to be an automaton, was it possible that this was how we all usually looked and sounded to Canopus: automata, bringing out these words or those, making these actions or those, prompted by shallow and surface parts of ourselves—for it was clear to me, as I stood there, that these demands and pleas were quite automatic, made by sleepwalkers. Even Alsi, who had had moments with me and with Johor of showing she knew quite well no such thing was going to happen, was leaning forward, asking with the others: "When, Johor? When?"

Johor said nothing, but gazed steadily back at them, and smiled a little.

And soon, in the same automatic, even indifferent way, they turned away from him, and began walking about the cleared space between the piles of dingy snow, and saying to each other: "Let us clear the snow away. How can the space-fleets land? There is nowhere for them to set themselves down." And they all began a hurrying scurrying activity, Alsi too, pushing the snow back off this space between the houses, piling it up, clearing paths—yet there was not room here for even Johor's Space Traveller to land comfortably, and certainly not one of the great interconstellation ships that would be needed to transfer large numbers. And yet there they all were, rushing about, working furiously, frowning, concentrated . . . and still I was seeing them as Johor must be—as if they had been set into action by some quite superficial and unimportant stimulus. I was watching Alsi most particularly, with sorrowful disbelief, but with a patient expectation that soon she would come to herself—and it struck me that this was the look I saw often on Johor's face as he watched me.

I said to him: "Very well, I understand, it is not yet time— though I don't know for *what* it isn't yet time."

We two were still standing quietly to one side, watching. We were not far from the shed behind the runs of the snow animals. We went there over the rutted and stained snow, past piles of the ice blocks that had the flowers and leaves of the summer plants, green and blue, frozen into them. The interior of the shed was crammed. Alsi had heaped it with sacks of the dried plant.

The floor of the shed was now iced over, and it was ice and not frost that gleamed from the low dried-plant ceiling. We sank into the sweet-smelling sacks, and pulled our coats close. A small white animal came running out from behind sack piles: Alsi had freed her pets into the shed, and they were living there, happily, and had bred, for some fluffy little beasts came out, looked at us, and chose the sacks we sat on as a playground. They had such confidence and such pleasure in everything, such charm—and what came welling up out of me was the cry: "And they will soon all be gone, all gone, and yet another species will have vanished from life and the living . . ." And I began on another cycle of pleas and of plaints, of grief—of sorrowing rebellion. "And what your answer will be I know, for there is no other; you will say, Johor, that this charm, this delightfulness, will vanish here and reappear elsewhere—on some place or planet that we have never heard of and that perhaps you have not heard of either! Charm is not lost, you say, the delicious friendliness that is the ground of these little animals' nature cannot be lost, for these are qualities that life must re-create—the vehicles that contain them, here, now, for us—yes, they will be gone soon, the little creatures will be dead, all of them, all—but we are not to mourn them, no, for their qualities will be reborn—somewhere. It does not matter that they are going, the individual does not matter, the species does not matter—Alsi does not matter, and nor does Doeg, nor Klin and Masson, nor Marl and Pedug and the rest, for when we are extinguished, then . . ." And as I reached this place in my chant, or dirge, I hesitated and my tongue stopped, hearing what I had said. I understood, yet did not, could not, yet.

I said, in the same thick, mechanical, even dead voice that I had heard used by the others outside, as they questioned Johor: "Yet we, the Representatives, we will be saved, so you say, I have been hearing you say—is that not what you said . . . yes, what else have you been saying . . . no, no, you have not said it, but then I haven't said anything like that either . . . yet if that is not what you have been meaning, intending me to hear . . ." I stopped my thick stupid mumbling and sat very quiet for a long time, a long long time. The little creatures tired of their tumbling play and lay close by me and Johor on the sacks, snuggling into the thick pelts. The two parents and four little ones, all licking our hands, sending out trills and murmurs of greeting, as to friends—their human friends. Soft blue eyes blinked at us, blinked more slowly, shut, opened showing the blue, then went out, as they slumbered there, curled into small white mounds.

I came out of the time of deep inward pondering which I was not able to monitor or direct, for it had its own laws and necessities, and I said: "I remember how the thought came into me that I, Doeg, was in the shape I am, with the features I have, because of a choice among multitudes. I set in front of myself a mirror, and I looked at my features—nose from my mother, eyes from my father, shape of head from one, set of body from the other, with memories of grandparents and great-grandparents. I looked, saying: her hands came down to him, and then to her and so to me, and his hair shows on that head and grew again on my grandmother, and so me—and I thought how that couple, my parents, could have given birth to—how many?—children, thousands, perhaps millions, every one slightly different—it was the slight difference that intrigued me in this private game of mine, and I imagined as I stood there looking at my face, my body, how stretching behind me, to each side of me, in every direction away from me, stood slight modifications of me, some very similar indeed, some hardly at all. I filled a town with these variations of myself, then a city, then, in my mind, whole landscapes. Doeg, Doeg, Doeg again, and mentally I greeted these nonexistent never-to-exist people, people who had not come into life because I had come in this precise shape of body and face, with this particular set of mannerisms—I said to these people, all of whom resembled me more or less, closely or only slightly, being the same height, or a little taller or a little shorter, with variations of the same hair, eyes in an allotment of possibilities—I said to them: Look, here you are, in me . . . for the feeling of me, of I, that feeling *I am here*, Doeg, would have been your feeling had the chances of the genes fallen differently, and if you, your particular shape and mould, had been born instead of me. What was born, then, to those repositories of a million years of the dicing of the genes, was a *feeling*, a consciousness, was the self-awareness: *here I am*. And this awareness was later given the name Doeg—though I have used many names in my life. That particular *feeling* was born into this shape and style and set of inherited attributes, and could have been born into any one of that multitude of others, the possibilities who, in my mind's eye, stand, and stood, like ghosts, smiling perhaps a little wryly, watching me who *chanced* to succeed. But they are me and I am them, for it was the feeling of me that was born . . ." And I lapsed out, went away then, for a time, and came back with: ". . . And yet you say, Johor, and of course, as soon as you say it, it is true, it must be true, that this precious thing, what I hold on to when I say: *I am here, Doeg,* this is the feeling I am, and have, and what I recognise in sleep, and will recognise as myself when I die, leaving all this behind, this precious little thing, so little, for awaking in a thick dark night out of a sleep so deep it takes a long time to know where and who you are, all there is of you, of your memories, of your life, of your loves, of your family and children and your friends—all that there is this little feeling, *here I am,* the feeling of *me*—and yet it is not mine at all, but is shared, it must be, for how can it be possible that there are as many shades and degrees of me-ness as there are individuals on this planet of ours? No, it must be that though I do not know it, this consciousness, *here I am, this is I, this is me,* this sensation that I cannot communicate to anyone, just as none of us may communicate to anyone else at all the atmosphere of a dream, no matter how familiar the dream, and how close it is to you, or how often it comes during a long life—this sensation, or taste, or touch, or recognition, or memory—this me-ness—is nevertheless known very well to others. But they may not know who else shares this particular taste or feel—this class or grade or kind of quality of consciousness. Meeting me, they do not know that I share what they are, their feeling of themselves; and I, meeting them, being with them, cannot know that we are the same. Nor can we know how many we are, or how few—nor how many grades or types or kinds of these states of consciousness there are. This planet of ours: are there a million different *me's* here? Half a million? Ten? Five? Or do we all share the same quality of self-consciousness? No, that is hard to believe—yet why not?—since we know so little of what we are, what, invisibly, we really are. It is as possible that there are a million different qualities of the consciousness that is all we are when we wake into a dark out of a deep sleep, and are unable to move for a while, let alone know where and why we are—as there are ten or five. But perhaps, Johor, when you look at this planet with your Canopus eyes, you do not see us as individuals at all, but as composites of individuals who share a quality that makes them, makes us, really, one. You look at us all and see not the swarming myriads, but sets of wholes, as we, looking into the waters of our lake, or up into the skies, saw there groups and swarms and shoals and flocks, each consisting of a multitude of individuals thinking themselves unique, but each making, as we could see with our superior supervising eyes, a whole, an entity, moving as one, living as one, behaving as one—thinking as one. Perhaps what you see of us is just that, a conglomerate of groups, or collectives, but these collectives need not be—it seems to me as I sit here thinking these thoughts, Johor, with you saying not a word—yet I would not be able to have these thoughts or anything like them were you *not* here—it seems to me that the wholes or groups or collectives need not be geographically close or contiguous, but that perhaps an individual who has precisely the same feeling of herself or himself as I do when waking in the dark out of a deep dream, knowing nothing of his or her past, or history, all memories gone too, for just that brief space—this individual might be one I never meet, might be living in a city on the other side of the planet where I have not been nor ever will go now. Might be someone, even, that I dislike, or have a repulsion for, just as easily as someone I feel drawn towards—for this business of antipathy and likeness is a chancy thing, and sometimes it is hard to tell the difference between attraction and repulsion, liking and disliking. But what a dimension that adds to the business of living, Johor, this idea of mine—*this idea of yours?*—that as I go about my work and my business, looking after this or that, doing what has to be done, meeting a hundred people in a day, then of these people it is possible I am meeting, not strangers, not the unknown, but *myself.* My self, all I know truly of myself, which is the feeling *here I am, I am here,*—all that is left of you when you wake in a thick dark with your limbs too weighty with sleep to move, and unable to remember what you are and what you are doing here or in what room you are waking. You said to me, Johor, that the terrible feeling of isolation and loneliness that comes over me when I understand that never, no matter how I tried, could I convey to any other being the atmosphere, the *reality,* the *real* nature of a dream landscape, those landscapes where we wander in our sleep and which are more real than our waking—this isolation must be softened, must be banished, by knowing that others, too, *must* use these landscapes in their sleep, and meet me there, as I meet them, though we will never, perhaps—or seldom—know it when we meet in the day, and so, too, my loneliness is softened when I reflect that in saying *I, here I am, here is what I am,* this feeling or sensation or taste of *me*—I speak for . . . but I do not know how many. For others, that is certain. In that feeling of me-ness, is, must be, a sharing, must be a companionship. I shall not ever again wake from the deep sleep, like black water, in which I have been so terribly and marvellously trustingly submerged—as trustingly as these small animals snuggle up to us, giving their helplessness and littleness to us, who are so enormous and unknown to them—without thinking, as I feel again, *Here I am, here is the consciousness of me,* of those others, who are I, are myself, though I do not know who they are, nor they me . . . it is a strange thing, Johor, to feel oneself part of a whole much larger than oneself, to feel oneself vanishing as one thinks, or talks, dissolving into some core, or essence—and that inner central place dissolving too, going away, changing as one talks, or thinks, or contemplates, into something else . . . what then am I, Johor, sitting here on this heap of half-frozen sacks that smell so deliciously of that lost summer of ours, my body so briefly at rest inside this great hide coat, my mind full of thoughts that come from somewhere, float around there, as if I am a sort of sieve or catchment for thoughts that are part of me for a time and then drift past? I look at you and know that in seeing an uncomfortable, rather unhealthy, and pallid personage, not very unlike myself, I see nothing at all of you, know nothing: know, only, because my mind tells me so, that this is Canopus—and that is so far beyond my conception that I have simply to let it go at that. I sense myself, think of myself; and as I do this I dissolve, go away, am left with nothing, nothing, nothing—unless I am the wind that blows through the immense spaces that lie between electron and electron, proton and its attendants, spaces that cannot be filled with *nothing,* since nothing is *nothing* . . ." And down I sank again into sleep, where a dark restfulness and reassurance always waited for me, and from which I drifted up again, back to the cold shed, with Johor there. He was watching the little animals, all awake again. They were pulling open a sack with their sharp white teeth to get at the contents, and scattering the dried sprays and pieces of green and faded blue about on the ice, and scampering about among them, and playing and rolling. He watched, and he smiled, and he smiled at me as I came up from the dark saying to myself, *Here am I, Doeg, and then: Here is the feeling of me that I share with my unknown friends, my other selves.*

Alsi was there too, so I saw then, sitting apart from us both. She was holding something between her large hands, which were ungloved, and bending forward over it, and mourning. One of the young animals was ill, or dying, and she was trying, with the vitality that still remained in her chilled hands, to revive it. She rocked as she sat, not knowing she did, back and forth, and from side to side, and I saw that this was a protest or a claim by her suffering much-tried body, a statement that a strong fighting life was still in it—just as much as it was an expression of the pain in her mind. And I thought again that bodies and minds were linked so closely, one affecting the other—yet in the wide spaces between the pulses that are the particles of the particles of the particles of the units of our physical being, there are no signs of—grief, for instance, or of love. Love, love, was grieving there in every small part of Alsi's large but gaunt body, for she knew, her terrible pain showed it was so, that this death meant others—the offspring of her two pets, these pretty delightful little babies, would soon be dead, for they could not endure their lives.

"Do you realise, Johor," she said to him, in the same heavy accusing way I sometimes used with him, "that there are no young things left with us on our planet? The calves born during the summer to the herds have died, they were not strong enough, and no more are being born—and outside there in the pens there are only adults. I cannot make them breed, nothing I do will change what they are feeling—or what they know." And she wept bitterly, her face close to the little furry creature in her cold hands, for it was quite dead, and stiffening.

Johor said nothing, but watched her.

When she had quietened herself, she said, still desperate, but in a low voice: "What are we going to do? When the herds are gone, and the adults of the snow animals gone—there will be nothing for us all to eat. Oh, I shall be glad, glad, for I am so sickened by this meat we have to eat that the last mouthful I have to force myself to chew will be a celebration for me—even if it means the end of me . . ." But here I could see some thought had struck her, for her face changed, and her eyes did not see us for a time, but the eyes of her mind looked inwards. She sighed at last, and came back to us. Carefully she laid down the heavy cold lump in her hands that had so recently been the delightful little animal playing around us, and she looked long and steadily at another that had stopped playing and was sitting shivering close to her foot. She bent, stroked it gently, and her face had sorrow hardened into it, but she did not pick it up.

"Alsi," said Johor, "I want you now to set aside Alsi and become Doeg." She looked at him. We often enough changed our roles, did different kinds of work: becoming for those times the Representative for whatever it was that was needed, so it was no new idea to her that she should "become Doeg," for she had "been Doeg" quite recently, when it was her turn to remember and to reproduce in words experiences that we all needed to have fixed and set so that our annals would be in order. She had told of the journey made up in the lands of the ice to the colder pole, standing among us Representatives, while we listened carefully; and while this was being done, she was Doeg.

"I want you to go back in your mind into your childhood, and tell of your feelings then, what you thought and how you saw your life." And he picked up one of the still healthy young animals, which at once started to lick and bite his fingers playfully and to rub its nose and face against them, and he sat there with it lightly caged, held before him on his knees. Its soft contented purring filled the icy shed, and its soft blue eyes blinked at us with the delighted recognition young things give to their discoveries: Oh, what a marvel this world is! How fantastic! Extraordinary! Wonderful! Look—what I can do with it! Watch me! And, held there among the thicknesses of Johor's coat, it put out a white paw to hook a flake of snow that had floated in somehow through the interstices of the roof, and then, as the flake vanished into the fur, the baby stretched and yawned, in a luxuriousness of pleasure in movement, and fell asleep as its muscles slackened, and dozed, in the most charming way, its chin on Johor's fingers.

Johor looked gently at the girl, whose eyes were running hot tears. She pushed the hood back off her face, feeling it confine her, and then in the same impulse shrugged the coat off her shoulders. Under it she wore layers of the worn and ragged clothes of our warm and smiling days; and these too her hands tugged and ripped as if on their impulse, not hers, and she was sitting there half-naked in her nest of shaggy pelts.

We did not see ourselves naked, these days; nor see the bodies of others. This was partly because of the terrible cold, and partly because of shame. I do not think that Alsi had intended to bare herself in this way, but she was being driven by grief. Her eyes were fixed on the little creature in Johor's hands, whose stillness now was not the moving breathing stillness of sleep, but had a stiffness about it. Her hands went out towards it in a wild unconscious gesture that said No, no, no,—I shall save you, and then withdrew themselves, and tugged again at her hair, and her eyes appeared in a fixed stare, between her fists.

"Alsi," said Johor—and laid down the little corpse beside him, on the frozen floor.

"I was born—born, but *I* cannot remember, and you know that, but I suppose I gave pleasure to everyone, as this little beast has just done to us, because of my charm and my unconsciousness of it. And I grew—but I don't remember how, but it was under your command and in your care, Canopus, since that is the essence of our life and our being. And I knew more and more of myself, thinking more often every day: *Here I am, this is Alsi*—and my feeling of myself was not in my body so much then, though I delighted in it, but somewhere else . . . perhaps in you, Canopus—but then, it is not for us to know, is it? But I remember how I would come to myself, a young child, filled with wonder, and delight, and marvelling, just as this poor dead thing was, until a moment ago. And then, suddenly, something else happened, my breasts appeared and . . ."

She sat staring in front of her a while, then her fists dropped from either side of her face, and her hands touched lightly just once the upper part of her chest, and then, in disbelief and repudiation, went lower . . . what we could see there was her rib cage, with the yellow skin stretched tight over it, each bone evident and—where were her breasts? Her hands crept lower, as her eyes were fixed, unconscious, ahead of her, and she pulled aside more garments and we saw that from the lower part of her chest two skinny bags depended, and these bags ended in small hard lumps, and on the skin that held the lumps were brown wrinkles—her nipples. She held these lumps in her large still strong hands, and then let them go, and explored with her hands her shoulders, where the bones and the joints showed clearly under stretched skin.

She was not weeping now, or grieving, but on her face was the look of one trying and trying to accommodate the impossible. The old, the very old woman's body, shrivelled by starvation, was displayed there before us, and her face was bare to us—gaunt, sallow, with sunken black eyes. Yet in the hollows near the sockets there was a vulnerability, something still fresh and youthful, and I was thinking, stoutly: Well, when we Representatives are all taken off here, and we eat again, as we need to eat, then Alsi will become a young woman, it is not too late and . . . But this thought sank away into the depths of my mind, and was not at ease there. No, I was thinking, no, that's not it, it is not—I must not make up these tales and fabrications, comforting myself, thinking how others must be comforted.

She put back the folds of her rags over the skin-covered bones, and pulled the thick coat around her again, and the hood down over her head, and was again not much more than strong dark eyes peering out from greasy shaggy hides.

"Alsi!" said Johor.

"Very well then! I was born . . . and now I shall die. No, Johor, if you want me to say how I see my life, then that is how, more and more often, I do see it . . . Tell me, when you look back along your life, do you—no, that is a useless question, I know it before I ask. You live so much longer than we do, it must seem to you when you look at us just as it seems to us when we look at these little creatures here whose lives are so short—or to them when they look at a snow-beetle! All the same I shall ask it, for it fills my mind, Johor, I cannot stop thinking and wondering about how you, you people with your Canopus minds, how do you experience your memories? For that is what you are wanting me to talk about now, isn't it? Memory, a thin transparent sort of stuff which is all that is left of a life when you have lived it? Do you feel as if your life has had no substance in it? No, of course you don't, but all the same I must ask. Do you feel as if you could blow aside your memories with a single strong breath? For that is how I see my life, like a scrap of cloth lying in a corner, or the fragment of a highly coloured web, the colours fading as I look: memory—memories, for there's nothing there of my life! Yes, I know I am going to die before I normally would, but if a life is something, then the third of a life is something and I am a third of the way through mine. It is nothing, my life, a little dream: I swear, Canopus, that when I come back into myself after a sleep, my dreams sometimes seem more vivid to me than my life does. *And yet*—here is where I have to ponder, and brood, and still make no sense of it all when I'm done with it—as I begin a day, it is like a hill I must climb, a weight I have to push uphill, something that has a weight of difficulty in it. Sometimes, as I wake, I cannot face the long heavy day ahead. Often, in the middle of a day, the thick dragging quality of it is such that it crushes me back into sleep again, even if only for a few moments, anything to lose the burden of being . . . conscious. Yes, of being awake to what is the texture and substance of a day—like a piece of cloth you weave, which may have patterns that you have chosen, but which you cannot choose *not* to weave, cannot refuse to finish, because this is a task which has been set. I stand sometimes in one of those pens out there, with the snow falling around me in one of its thousand ways—light or thick, and blowing sideways or straight or wet or dry, or in crumbs or the large soft masses flakes make when they are clinging together—I look, and I feel as if every step I take to here, where the food is, and the task of carrying it all out and spreading it about, and then checking on how the snow-beasts are, and how many, and if any have died . . . all this is so difficult, Johor, it is as if every atom of my body is being held in a force. And yet I do it—and having done it, I say: That's done,

I've accomplished that, I've finished that task, and the next task lies ahead—collecting the others who make up Alsi to gather food for the beasts, or whatever is the next thing that has to be done. All day, one burdensome effort after another; and then the day is finished, and the blessed night is here, and I look back at the day— and it's gone! A little coloured smear of thought, a few pictures running together, a scene of me standing in a pen, with the animals gathering around waiting to be fed, or me walking with hunched shoulders through a blizzard, and perhaps the sensation of cold around my neck or numbed chilled feet. A day! The memory of a day! A day that was so hard to accomplish, and when it is done— nothing! A life . . . the memories of a life. Surely, Canopus, there is something here that is out of phase, out of a proper fitting to- gether? It seems to me more and more impossible, wrong, that the actual doing of a thing, the living it, has as its shadow so fleeting and faint a record: memory. And I ask myself more and more, is this why we need Doeg? What is Doeg but an attempt, and even a desperate and perhaps a tragic attempt, to make the faint coloured shadow, memory, stronger? Give our memories more substance? Is that what Doeg is—and why you want me, now, at this time, to be Doeg?"

"I am not sure what your name is, when you ask these questions, but it is not Doeg!"

She smiled here, acknowledging what he said, and sat quietly for a time, thinking.

"Very well," she began again, "but it seems to me that what I have to remember is so—*nothing*, Johor; and it is all over, gone under the ice . . . When I came to be aware of myself, when I en- tered into the feeling, *here I am*, I was with my parents in our house. You came to our house once. It was in a little town, one of a group of small towns, all occupied with the production of cloth. Each town was known for something. Our town actually wove the cloth. The town across the valley made the machinery that made the cloth. On the other side of our hill was a town where everyone was involved with the production of dyes. Some were natural, which we had discovered for ourselves from plants and clays and rocks, but others were artificial, and it was Canopus who made us think in ways that led to the discovery of how to evolve dyes. Another town nearby made all kinds of yarns and threads. The cluster of towns grew like this, nothing was planned—and now when I think of all that time, what distinguished it was a naturalness in the way things grew and happened. But there was a change, wasn't there, Johor? There was a point when our lives, instead of being a function of what was around us, growing out of what was there, became more . . . conscious, is that the word? Can we use that word for a collective way of looking at—"

"Alsi," said Johor.

"Yes. Very well. I grew as all children did then. We learned everything we had to know from the adults around us. And now I *have* to make the comment that it was unconscious, Johor! Both on the part of the children, and on the part of the adults! That was before Pedug came . . ."

"No, before Pedug felt that a name was necessary."

She thought about this, and soon nodded. "Yes. For of course children have to be taught what is necessary—and what is necessary has to change. All the adults were Pedug, for children learned, as naturally as they breathed, from the adults. But then there was a change, and it was when you, Canopus, brought the instrument that made small things visible—yes, Canopus, that was when a certain kind of naturalness and pleasantness ended. It was not just that you brought only a few of these instruments, for of course you could not bring one for every household, or even one for every town! No, you brought us as many as you could, but for every person on our planet to look, and to learn what it is we are really made of, the instruments had to be carried around from place to place. By Pedug. And for the first time children and young people left the circle of their parents and friendly adults and gathered together, as children being taught, at a particular time and in a particular place, and sat around Pedug and were instructed. And what an extraordinary, what an absolutely fundamental change that was, Johor! And of course you knew it was, and had calculated it all, and understood that what was happening must change the way we all looked at ourselves. For, once, children never left their own parents and relatives and friends, all of whom were responsible for them, and hardly knew what it was they were learning, for it was taken in everywhere, all the time, in every possible way. I, for instance, who know all there is to know about the processes of making cloth, don't know how I learned it! But when I sat in a large space, listening to Pedug who made me apply my eyes to the instrument, and made me look at what was there, and made me think about it—oh, then, Johor, indeed everything was changed. We became conscious that we were learning, and of how we learned . . . and this was at the same time as we saw the substance of our bodies, and found that it vanished as we looked, and knew that we were a dance and a dazzle and a continual vibrating movement, a flowing. Knew that we were mostly space, and that when we touched our hands to our faces and felt flesh there, it was an illusion, and that while our hands felt a warm solidity, in reality an illusion was touching another illusion—and yet, Johor, in all my life, which of course is going to be so short, and perhaps does not deserve the name of a life at all . . . but you are going to say that I have gone off again, I've not stuck to the point, I'm not doing what you ask! But Johor, isn't that in itself an illustration of what I am saying to you? I simply cannot keep my mind on what seems like a short and—at least at the beginnings of it—delightful dream . . ."

"You lived with your parents in a house in . . . ?"

"I was born in Xhodus, which was one of four small towns that together made cloth. While I was small my parents were both employed in the processes of weaving, though later both became Pedug and were often away from home, travelling around our planet with the new instrument, teaching the new ways of seeing and thinking. I had two brothers and two sisters, and we were all learning the skills of our group of towns. As for me, during the time when my parents were taking me into all kinds of places and situations to find out what my nature was, I was taken to a farm, an hour's walking away, that produced fleeces for our cloth makers. I and my parents and the other children lived for some weeks on that farm, but my brothers and sisters were not attracted to any of the kinds of work there, while I was. I told my parents that I wanted to be Alsi, to be one of those who were engaged with the nurture of growing animals. And that is what I became, very young, for I often visited there, and agreed to be apprenticed when the time came at that farm, and expected to spend my life there. But then the cold came . . . and now all that life, the towns, the animals, the trees —all, everything, gone under deep ice. And I see it like this, that a dream lies there under the ice, something that had no substance to it; and yet it was life, was living, was a long, complex process of living that . . . But it was a good and real and honest life, wasn't it, Johor? Nothing that we need to be ashamed of now? Though that is an absurd way of talking, for how can one be ashamed of something one has not *chosen*—we did not choose our lives or how we evolved, how we changed. For we were changing, I know that now, even before you brought the instrument that we all had to look through and find that our selves, that the ways we experienced ourselves, were all illusion. And perhaps those changes were not all good? How can we say now? *For I cannot properly remember!* I talk to others who were young with me—those of us who are still alive, that is, or who still move around upright trying to work in spite of the blizzards and the storms—and we all remember different things. Isn't that strange, Johor? And so while we all agree that, yes, there were changes, and that these changes could be described by saying that an innocence was going from our lives, by saying that there was a new kind of self-consciousness, even before the new instruments came, we cannot agree at all about what these changes were. I say, Do you remember this and that? And they say, No, but surely you remember . . . ? Johor, there is something intolerable here, you must see this? Must agree? Must—"

"Alsi," said Johor.

"Yes. The house that I was born in was like all our houses then. We would make a house in a few days, and perhaps a hundred people would come and help. We had feasts and festivals when we decided it was time for a new house. A house could be entirely of reeds or slats of thin wood held together on string. Roofs and walls were always moveable, so we could open and close them as the winds altered or if it rained. A house then changed all through the day, walls being lowered and lifted, roofs being tied back, and people came and went all day and all night too, for we did not have any rigid ordinances about when we had to sleep, day or night.

It was a communal life, and a flexible one, and it was easy, and we were easy with each other—for I have noticed that since the cold, and the difficulties we have now, we are hard on each other, and we criticise and make demands, and punishments come easily to our minds though they never did before. That was what I think of most in our old life, how fluid it was, how adaptable, houses and streets and towns changed as plants do, turning towards or away from light. How we would pull a house down one day, and the next another went up. How on the farm we moved the enclosures for animals around, daily, it seems now; how even storehouses and places that had to have some sort of solidity were always being rebuilt. And yet I remember, too, how when the new building went up for the machinery that had just been invented to weave cloth more quickly, we all stood around it and felt uncomfortable and threatened. This was not one of the familiar buildings, all lightness and slatted shadows and breezes blowing, that we could pull into a new shape by tugging a rope or pushing across a screen; no, it was built of stone and earth and had a thick roof, so that the old way of living of ours was already challenged, before the cold, before The Ice, and I wonder—"

"Alsi, describe yourself, as if you were someone else, as if you were telling a story. Take some incident you remember, any incident."

"An incident you want, Johor! A little tale! How I fear these little incidents our memories store up! In our house came to live my father's mother and my mother's father—these two old people had to be listened to, every day, by somebody. We used to take turns to listen, as a task. For what was remembered was always the same. Both these old people would sit there—not together, for the old woman liked the sun and the old man chose a shady place, and in any case old people like the company of the young and not of each other—they sat there, and when one of us went to listen, out came exactly the same incidents, in the same words—a life. A string of a few incidents, always the same. We children would listen to these same words for the tenth, then the hundredth, then the thousandth time. A life. What was eaten on a certain day, nearly a hundred years before. What another had said fifty years ago. Over and over again. Memory . . . And so now you want me to create a memory that I will bore my grandchildren with—but of course I am not going to have any, so I am safe! Very well, Johor. I came from the farm one warm and pleasant evening, to visit my family, and on the way something happened I did not expect. I had not gone more than a few minutes' walking from the farm when I saw in front of me . . . I see myself walking there, a girl of about twelve. She is a tall child, rather scrawny, and she is wearing a bright green cloth tied around her waist, and a red cloth over her breasts which have just begun to show. She is carrying a present for her parents from the farm, of some dressed meat. The meat attracts some birds that gather in the air above her. At first she does not notice them but walks along, swinging her basket and very proud of how she looks in her new coloured cloths and her new points of breasts. Suddenly she sees shadows moving fast all around her on the path and on the grass, and she looks up and sees hanging in the air just above her the great birds, their talons bunched up under them, their beaks pointing down. She shouts up at them, and hears her voice thin and reedy, and hears the loud scream of a bird, and an answering scream from another. The birds are flapping now around her head, trying to frighten her. She feels the hot breeze on her cheek made by the wings, smells the warm rank smell. She will not give up her basket, she will not; and then a bird comes straight into her face, and alights for just a moment on her head. She can feel the sharp talons in her scalp, and she drops the basket and runs off, and looks back to see three birds settling around the meat that has spilled out of the basket. She yells at them all kinds of abuse, You filthy greedy beasts, you horrible things—and they are off into the blue air, their claws full of red lumps of meat, and her basket is lying empty and on its side in the brown dust. She picks up the basket and walks on home with it, already framing in her mind the words she will use to tell her parents about it—and because she did that, made the effort to choose the right words that would make of her plight there along the road between farm and little town a sympathetic and interesting thing, so that they all, parents, siblings, grandparents, friends, neighbours would come close and listen and perhaps say Poor Alsi, you must have been frightened—

because of that, the incident stuck in the girl's mind, so that she can see it as clearly as if she were standing on the side of the road watching the young girl come jauntily along in her bright colours, and how the great birds came together overhead, and conferred and then allowed themselves to sink through the warm air till they were just above the girl, ready to beat and battle with their strong spread wings."

"Go on from there, Alsi. Remember what happened when you did get home, and when you had told your tale and the people who had listened had turned their attention to something else? Can you remember how . . ."

But I did not hear any more of Alsi's efforts with memory, for the door opened in a screech of wind and a messenger came in, from Bratch for me: my aid was needed. I was to become Bratch for a time, as Alsi had become Doeg, and I went out into the wind that was coming straight down from the lands above our wall in a continuous driving squall.

I stumbled through the loose drifts, holding on to the young woman who had come to fetch me, as she clung to me, and in this way we forced our way out beyond the edges of our town and into the empty tundra where nothing could be seen but the driving snow, and so, slowly and painfully, towards the next town.

By the time we reached there, the blizzard had ceased. This town when we came on it was near obliterated, the snows had been so heavy. We pushed our way through the thick loose choking snow, well above the level of the first layer of windows where, in some places, we could see movements and pushings as if creatures were everywhere struggling out of eggs. We came to a building where the snow was smooth and thick to the height of the first ceiling, but there was a tunnel excavated down to the door, and we went down that, into a room used for meetings and discussions, and now filled with people who were sitting—not lying in that half-death of lethargic sleep—and waiting for me and for others from near towns. For there was a new danger, which soon I saw for myself, for the whole company of us went out into a morning where a cold and pale sun shone distantly in a pale hazy sky. But our eyes were not directed upwards to this rare enough sight—sun, in an unclouded sky—but on the wall that ran just beyond the edge of this town. Above it reared the familiar savage crests and shelves of ice; but the wall itself was cracked from top to bottom, black on white, for the inside of the wall had not yet frosted and dimmed. That sharp bright black astonished our eyes, and we stood staring, and as we did the crack widened, in a groan, and chips of ice flew everywhere, even threatening our poor exposed faces, and clouds of snow fell from the top of the wall. And suddenly the wall itself bulged, and then the upper part of it was crushed under the awful weight of the ice above, and fell almost to where we stood, and the ice sheets protruded forward and ground down the wall still further— and then we were standing in the little central square of the town, with the glacier coming right into it. The wall at that place did not exist—had gone.

We all knew what would happen, and what the danger to our people was: for before they had sent for me and for the others who would become Bratch for a time, they had already been into all the dwellings of the town, urging the inhabitants to come out, and to make new plans for themselves, to move away from this now dangerous wall. But they would not move, could not be made to rouse themselves. The stores of stimulant frozen water, with the flowers and leaves shining in it, were neglected, and in any case only the few already active ones had made use of them.

We had to make them all wake up and come out of the dark caves their dwellings now were, and to think how to make new shelters, and quickly, for we could hear the groaning and screaming of the ice as it pushed and slid above us towards the weak place in our wall, which was collapsing fast and faster on either side of the gap that was now filled completely with ice.

Our problem, worse than how to get new shelters built, was the fear in our minds. For something new, and impossible and deadly had happened—Canopus had been wrong, had said something which had then been cancelled, negated. The wall, our wall, which had absorbed so much of our strength and our substance, which was there because of Canopus—and which was built exactly according to the minutest prescriptions of Canopus—was breached, was down, and if in this place, then it was almost certainly down in other places, which we had not yet heard about—and probably would not, since travel now was so difficult and slow. The wall had been there to save us from the ice, and this was because Canopus would come and take us all away to the lovely Rohanda, our paradise, whose mother star we had often sought out in the sky, and then admired with our eyes and with our minds. But the wall was not going to save us . . . and Canopus, in the shape of Johor, a half-starved, half-frozen creature like ourselves, sat in a heap of dirty heavy hides in a shed, talking to poor Alsi, who was being Doeg—but why, what for, why, why, why—*why was he troubling at all?*—that was what had to be in our minds, then, as we stood looking up at where the ice had pushed our invulnerable, unconquerable wall over and down. If the wall had gone down under the onslaughts of the ice, then Canopus had made a mistake, and that meant . . . and those among us, Representatives and the represented, who had been talking—though less and less—about paradises and rescue and the fleets of spaceships which would soon, very soon, arrive and whisk us all away, fell silent, no longer spoke of rescue . . . yet, in spite of the despondency and despair which every one of us now felt, and knew we all felt, it was necessary to confer, to measure our situation, and to rouse those slumbrous dazed ones who could not or would not rouse themselves. *But what for?* In our hearts now we all knew, every one, that they would be roused and stimulated—if we could achieve this—to no end, for the space-fleets would not be coming. Yet Canopus wanted this. Johor said this most clearly and definitely. As long as it was possible, he wanted every individual up and alert, instead of drowsy and unconscious. And while we could see no sense in it, even a sort of cruelty, since the sleep and the lethargy were for protection, and because the people did not want to face what was happening—we had to do what he wanted. What Canopus wanted . . .

We, the alert among us, left the central place in the town which was being so horribly threatened by the glacier, and went back into the space under the snows, and we sat there, eating our little ration of dried meat, and we thought of how to get everyone awake and working. We had no resources but the small stores of ice that had the principle of the summer plant in it, and since that was all we could think of, knowing that exhortations on the lines of "Canopus says . . ." were now useless, we set ourselves to chipping the blocks of ice into smaller and smaller pieces. These we piled on to trays, and a piled tray was carried by a team into every one of the dark odorous caves under the snows. I, carrying this desperate medicine— I, as Bratch—went into a room with others, who were Bratch, and we aroused the sleepers, and, as each one groaned awake, an arm across eyes unaccustomed now even to the little glimmer of light we brought in with us from the pallid outdoors, we held them up, and pushed the ice chips into their mouths and made sure the water was swallowed. And as animation came into their faces, and their struggles against us became stronger, we hauled them up, and pushed them up steps, and then up through the snow masses that covered the dwellings, into the central place of the town where the ice-tongue was protruding. Crowds of these poor wretches stood blinking there, up at the collapsed wall—which could not collapse, since Canopus had ordered it, but had collapsed—and then at how the glacier inched forward. They stared, and turned their heads listlessly about—for the animation the water had fed into them was not much—and most showed signs of wanting to stumble back under the snow into their sleep again. How strong is that deep, dark drive towards sleep, towards death, towards annihilation; how terribly, fearfully strong it is, and in every one of us—for I have felt it, as they did. I have lain drugged by my own indifference under the piled hides, and was saved only because others shook me awake and fought with me and made me struggle up into the cold light. To get them to move then, and to stand long enough for the active principle of the liquid to sting all their tissues awake— this was what we had to do, and we did, though we were using all our strength, physical and moral, to keep them from going back and down into the dark. We fought with them, and soon teams of them were at work dragging, on sledges and on anything that would slide over the snow, shovels and spades and the dried meats and the hides, out of that town, well clear of it, where we could build some shelters with the snow itself, for there was nothing else. The listlessness of them!—the dulled confusion!—their indifference! We had to fight, and exhort, and support. Long lines of its inhabitants stumbled away from their town, kept up this heavy staggering movement until night came and with it another blizzard. But we made them move on, and in the morning it was a clear day, not snowing, though the clouds were low and fast and thick over us, and again we walked through the day, and that night we were aided by a sky where we saw, very faint and distant and often obscured by cloud, some stars. And these encouraged us, and kept us moving. Next day, being at what we judged a safe distance, we made little houses of piled snow and blocks of ice, each one approached by a long tunnel through which one had to crawl. And in each were piles of hides, and small glimmering lights made of tallow from the herds, and stores of dried meats. And into each went four or five or more people, collapsing back at once into their lethargy, for the effect of the stimulant was wearing off. They were alive: were safe—for a time. For as long as was necessary . . . *necessary for what?* And the teams of us, of Bratch, made sure that in each shelter was one more energetic and lively than the others, though that was not saying much; and laid upon each the responsibility of seeing that the inhabitants of the snowhouses must be awake part of the time, must not be allowed to slide into the last sleep of all. Must not, must *not*—and when their eyes searched ours, with *Why, what is the use?* we put into our own eyes assurance and confidence we did not feel—for we did *not* feel ourselves able to say: Because Canopus says so.

And leaving this little settlement half buried in snow, we went off into the town nearest this on the side away from that where Johor still sat listening to Alsi as Doeg; and found there that the wall was holding, though the ice was rearing up over it so fearfully that it could not hold long. And again we started on the wearing dragging painful business of rousing people up, and making them move out, and build themselves shelter.

And when that town was evacuated and the people "safe"—as far as was possible—we went to the next . . . and the next . . . where we met Bratch again, Bratch the physician, at the work of rousing and reassuring, for all long the wall black cracks had appeared, and then the wall had collapsed and the ice had come pushing through, and people were being moved out of their towns farther away from the lands of the ice above the wall. And so we all laboured, teams of us, very many of us: we, Bratch, worked at saving minds and bodies. And there was not one of us who did not ask silently and secretly: Why? What for? Since these people will die here, in their snow huts, and only a little later than they would if they had been left in their own places and towns. For it is only we, the Representatives, that will be saved . . . but this thought, I could see, did not take root in them, the Representatives, just as, in me, it could not find a home, but was rejected, presenting itself back to my conscious thought as something refused. No, it was not a lack of justice that we rejected—that we, the few, should be saved when the others would not be, but would be entombed in a planet of ice—for *justice* is something not so easily understood. It was, quite simply, that there was something in the *substance* of the thought, in its texture and quality, that could not find acceptance in our minds. In our new minds—for we understood that everything in us was new, being new-made, new-worked, changed. While we laboured and fought and exhorted and forced the doomed wretches up and out of their saving kindly lethargy, we were being changed, molecule by molecule, atom by atom. And in the unimaginably vast spaces between the particles of the particles of the particles of the electrons and neutrons and protons—between the particles that danced and flowed and vibrated? Yes, in these faint webs or lattices or grids of pulses, changes went on over which we had no control. Which we could not chart or measure. Thoughts—but where were they, in the empty spaces of our beings?—that once we had regarded tolerantly, or with approval, as necessary, were now being rejected by what we had become.

When we had shepherded the people of yet another town, or city, or village out and away from the deadly wall which the ice was crushing, and into the white wilderness where only tiny ice huts sheltered them from the blizzards, and where they would be engulfed, sooner or later—then we were not able to see that our situation was any different from theirs. Both kinds of us, the people of Planet 8, the represented and the Representative—endured. The thought in our minds was that they were being changed by what we were forced to do; that we were being changed by their being made to stay alive when they would so very much rather have drifted away from our common effort into death.

So we employed ourselves, we, the Representatives, who were sometimes Bratch the physician, and sometimes Zdanye, those who sheltered and protected—for we did not think that we might properly use the word Masson, the builder, in connection with this work we did, of causing little huts of snow and ice to be made. Yet we did wonder if, in a world of only snow and ice—for we could believe that in the vastnesses of our galaxy such planets existed—whether the inhabitants could come to live with contentment, not knowing better. Those of us who had been taken to other planets in the course of our education as Representatives had seen such variety, such extremes, such unexpectedness, that we could believe there were beings who rejoiced in their icy worlds, as we had done once in the sunlit and favoured lands of our planet, where if cold winds blew this was enough of an event to make tales of it for our children. Yes, I could remember Doeg—my parents, older people, travellers—beginning a chronicle with, "And so, my friends, you must imagine that on that day a very cold wind came fast across the sky, blowing the clouds together and apart, blew so strongly across our ocean that there were waves the height of small hills—yes, it is true, it was so. And then . . ." And the thoughtful eyes of the young people . . .

While we were engaged in this work of moving the people, news came that our ocean—our little lake—was freezing so deep that it was no longer easy to find in it what food remained there. I went with some others, as Rivalin the Lake Guardians, through long slow snowfalls, which lessened as we went down and away from the middle lands until we were in a grey wilderness of hills and valleys, with the lake a white hard gleam, and we averted our eyes from it as much as we could, for white, white, white had again filled our minds and sight till we felt our thoughts were being blinded by its never-endingness. Yes, even these greys and the frosted rocks, and the soil that was brown and speckled with white crystals, were a rest to us; and so we came stumbling to the lake where we could see, far out in its centre, a small dark crowding activity, a bustle, which had about it a frantic urgency, and we walked out on the slippery ice, without thinking that we had never done this before, until we saw that a large hole had been cut in the ice, the size of a pond, black rocking sloshing water in a rigid white casing, and on this balanced most dangerously small boats that had lines and nets over their sides. All around this hole, whose sides were more than the height of the tallest among us, stood those whose task it was to break up the ice as the water kept thickening, and making a skin, and then flakes, and then thin sheets of ice. But the water was freezing faster than it was possible to break up the crust.

From the boats sparse loads of sea creatures were shovelled up on to the ice, and dragged away on sledges. Very thin supplies these were—the last of our food from our ocean. And I saw how some took up these still wriggling little water-things, which were fighting for their lives in the freezing air, and bit into them when hunger for freshness overcame them and overrode everything that was in them of restraint and abstention. I, too, was filled with a gnawing painful need for this food, and I felt myself being drawn across the ice to the edges of the pond, my hands out, my mouth filled with need, already tasting the crunching salty freshness—but I was brought to a halt before I took one up off the ice and bit into it. And others too, like myself, stumbled towards the food, but stopped, and we were all thinking of those starving in their ice houses, or going about their work, starving.

But what lay about us on the ice verges was not going to keep life in more than a few for a very short time—and, as we stood there, the sky came low in a smother of white, the snow began to fall, whitening the black of the water, and then there was no black, but a whirling black-and-grey, and, very soon, the water hole, or pond, was crusted over, and the boats were held fast. The people working in the boats were just visible as they put their feet out over the edges, to test the new ice, and stood on it, and then ran quickly across it, for it bent and squeaked under them, to the edges where they had to jump up again and again till their hands could find a hold on the ice cliffs, and we could haul them up. And there we all stood, for the last time as Rivalin the Custodians of the Lake; there we stood a long time, thinking of our sacred waters, under the ice, and what few creatures remained there sealed in, with the suffocating cold above them, and the white coming lower and lower, cramming them down and pushing them into the muddy bottom, and killing them as all their waters froze.

It seemed then, as we turned to go back, that in front of us the whole sky had become a wall or cliff of frozen water, for it was stifling white from the zenith to our feet, and as we stared forward into it we could see nothing, not even the towering breaking crest of the wall. Many of us were thinking that there was no purpose in walking back into that freezing smother of white, that inevitable death. But we did walk on, and on, and when we came to the first cluster of little ice huts, and crawled into one, coughing and blinking our eyes because of the greasy smoke from the burning fat, a face appeared from the heap of skins, and a voice said: "Someone came. It is time the Representatives went down to the pole. It is summer again there." And the speaker coughed, and the face went again in the dimness, under a shaggy sleeve, and we crawled out backwards along the ice tunnel, and stood all together in a hollow in the storm, and thought of the blue flowers and soft sappy greens of the summer that had gone. We found the sledges that had had the dead sea-things on them, and we sent messengers up into the blizzards to say that supplies of the magical blue plant were being sought for—and fifty of us Representatives travelled down, down, to seek for the summer. Again we travelled in the low space between a pressing white smother of cloud and the billowing white of the land, the wind at our backs, and again we huddled together through the dark nights, inside caves of snow we made for ourselves as the light went. And it seemed to us that the dreadful dark of the nights was shorter, and we felt that soon we would reach the summer lands. We were looking ahead, as we reached each rise or hill, with all the strength of our eyes and our minds, trying to penetrate the obliterating white, to see if there, at last, the sky would show a gleam of blue, or even of a lighter grey. But then we knew that we had passed beyond where, last season, the snows had ended and the open tundra had begun. Still snow encompassed us. Still we laboured on till from the top of a mountain, we saw the pillar, or spire, or column that marked the pole, and around it, but not for very far, was the greyish green of the moorland. And there were no flowers, no plant life, at all. Nor was there any sign of the herds. But we did not have the moral energy to wonder about the herds, for what we were facing, we knew, was the end of the planet. This was where we had, finally, to accept the end of our shifts and contrivances and our long endurances. When we reached where the snow became thin, or lay in wet yellowish banks and shoals, like coarse damp sand, and became only streaks and spots on soaked grass and on bogs—there we settled ourselves, trying to feel that the distant sun had some strength in it. We looked ahead across a day's walking distance to the tall column, and all we could see was the dark earth with sometimes a little dull green, or a smear or stain of grey.

We had very little to eat, only a few pieces of dried meat. But we did not want to eat. It was as if, while we few waited there, not knowing what we were to think or plan for, we had already gone beyond the need to eat, or to work for sustenance, or to maintain our pitifully depleted and deprived bodies that shivered inside the dense hide coats we had not removed—for it was not warm enough to do without them. Our eyes were drawn to the tall slender spire of the column that Canopus had set there, and had used for so long as a guide for their craft. Its absolute perfection of proportion, its balance, even the way it had been set in a certain relation to the slope of hills and the sky, spoke of Canopus, Canopus—and not of this planet; and what was in all our minds as we waited there, gazing at the thing, was only Canopus, who was coming to save us.

Yet I knew very well that there were no space-fleets coming in— I knew it now as I had not before, with a quiet and definite conviction, which was giving birth to—yes, hope; but of a kind that was unfamiliar to me. To believe, as we had, and for so long, or at least with part of our minds, that one day our skies would flash and shine everywhere as they filled with the Canopean fleets, and that *then* all our suffering populations would find safety "in the stars"—that was a resting on the future. But it was not a future that had any continuance with our past. It was a real and complete change that took place in me then, as I finally relinquished the old hope and dream, and looked steadily at the perfection of that tall black spire there, which still reflected lights from the sky, just as our wall had once done when it was clean and unfrosted. Inside me was some small spring of strength and self-reliance that I felt to be indestructible, and becoming stronger. This strength was what I was—I, Doeg; and across it, as clouds or birds traverse a sky not changing it at all, went thoughts and emotions. Among them, but very faint and even rather ridiculous was the familiar: *One day Canopus will come and save us* . . . And it seemed that when I looked into the faces of my friends, faces known to me as well as my own; into their eyes, which sometimes seemed to me as much mine as theirs—that I was seeing there what I knew to be true of myself. Even as one might say: "Perhaps they will come tomorrow!" and another answered: "Or the day after, or next week—the summer still has days or weeks to live!"—it seemed that these words were coming out of a superficial part of them, and that they were not even fully aware of what they said. I could see from their eyes that their minds were occupied with quite other kinds of thought, or speculation, or—even—conviction.

It is a very remarkable thing how ideas come into a mind, or minds: one minute we are thinking this or that, as if no other thought is possible to us; shortly after, there are quite different beliefs and possibilities inside our heads. Yet how did they get there? How *do* they arrive, these new notions, thoughts, ideas, beliefs, dispossessing the old ones, and to be dispossessed, of course, soon enough in their turn?

I knew, as we all waited shivering inside our coats, with the faint pale sunlight on our faces, that while my companions muttered: Canopus will come, we shall be saved—and the other shreds and pieces of our old dreams—changes were going on inside them that they were not conscious of.

And so we stayed there, being together on the hillside that had patches of grass and low tough plants on it, with the snowy lands behind us from where drove harsh and bitter winds. Nor did any of us show any disposition to move, or to talk of our responsibilities to our populations, or to discuss what we ought to do—whether to go in search of the vanished herds, or to send messages about their disappearance, or any of the other things that normally would have driven us up and into activity.

We were watching not only the dreary spaces of moor and tundra around the column but, more than these, each other. Increasingly, our eyes were on each other, searchingly, patiently—as if we did not know every one of us, as in fact we did; so very well that we could at any moment take on each other's work and—in a sense—become each other. We gazed close into eyes and faces as if there was very much more to be learned there than we had ever believed. And, soon, we were all in a rough circle, looking in and not out at the little spaces of our "summer." We faced inwards, as if the truth available to us was there, between us . . . in us . . . among us. In our being there together, in that way, in our extremity.

And so, later, were we found by Alsi and Johor who came out of the white wilderness towards us, showing by the way they stumbled and slid over the roughnesses of the ground how exhausted they were. And they flung themselves down among us, and lay there, eyes closed. And we saw how the yellow skin stretched over the bones of their faces.

We waited until Alsi opened her eyes and sat up, and Johor did the same.

I said to her, "And how was it with you, as Doeg?" She said, smiling, "Doeg, it seemed to me that as I spoke, everything that had happened to me, all my thoughts and my feelings, everything that I believed I had to be, was being put together in words, words, words—parcelled up, packaged up, and sent away . . . yes Doeg, I-Doeg—saw Alsi doing this and that, feeling thus or thinking so— and who was Alsi? I watched her, saw myself moving there among all the others . . . and now, I look back at myself as Doeg sitting in the shed with Johor, I see myself there, and see Johor, two people sitting together talking. And who was Doeg? Who, Doeg, is Doeg? And where now are Alsi or Doeg—for what is left of us all now? And to whom will you or I or any one of us be telling our little tales, singing our little songs?" And she looked, smiling, at me, and then at Johor who was listening as he lay propped on his elbow, and then at all the others. Slowly she looked at one after another, and we all looked back at her. When Alsi came back to us, with Johor, our small assembly of people had been made even more sharply aware of ourselves, our situation. We *felt* ourselves, as sharply as we saw—on a cold hillside, under a low cold hurrying sky, half a hundred individuals sitting together, fifty heaps of dirty shaggy animal skin and inside each a shivering parcel of bones and flesh, and thoughts and feelings too (but where were they, what were they?). We huddled there, listening to how the blizzards on the horizon squealed and raged and threatened this brief summer of ours which was no more than a small space or time at the very extremity of our planet, for the frosts of the approaching winter were beginning to show themselves. White on black, small white particles on black soil, crumbs and crystals of white scattered on the rocks and the grey-green grasses and on the wiry little plants— and in the air around us white flakes, only a few still, drifting, catching the weak sunlight, floating and sinking to settle with the frost on the earth. High above us, under heavy white clouds that had black crevasses, circled the great birds of the snow, white on white.

"If you are no longer Alsi," I said to her, "that means the snow animals are dead?"

"The pens are empty now, all of them."

We all looked, and then understood that this was what we were doing, at her hands: those knots of thin bones that had once been so large and so capable, tending so well the small, the weak, the vulnerable.

And *she* was looking at Johor. And that was a look not so easily described. For one thing, there was nothing in it of suppliance. Or even of need. What was there, and most strongly, was the recognition of him, of Canopus.

"I am no longer Alsi," she said to him. "Not in any way, or in any capacity." This sounded almost like a question; and in a moment she answered it. "Somewhere else there is Alsi—another place, another time. Alsi cannot disappear since Alsi is and must be continually re-created." Again she seemed to wait for him to speak, but he only smiled. "Though we cannot see them, since it is day now, and the sunlight up there obscures this truth, our sky is full of stars and planets and on them there is Alsi, Alsi—there I am, since it must be so."

"Since it must be so," voices echoed her from our group.

"So, since this is not Alsi, who am I, Johor, *and what is my name?*"

I said to him: "Doeg tells tales and sings songs in all times and all places, everywhere people use sounds to communicate, so if I am no longer Doeg, then Doeg still is, and perhaps as the dark comes down . . ."—and it was coming down, as we talked, and small distant stars appeared—". . . we are looking as we raise our eyes at worlds where Doeg is at work, for Doeg has to be. But who am I, Johor, and what is my name?"

And then Klin, the Fruit Maker, the Guardian of the Orchards: "There is not one orchard or fruit tree or fruit anywhere in this world of ours, nothing is left of all that beauty and richness—and so Klin I am not, since Klin was what I did—Klin is at work somewhere else, there Klin grafts shoots to shoots, Klin buds and blends and makes, and causes branches to lie heavy with blossom and then with fruit. But not here, not anywhere here, and so I am no longer Klin. And what is my name?"

And Bratch: "The skill in my mind and in my hands is at work now, at work everywhere there are creatures of flesh and sinew, and blood and bone—Bratch is needed, and so Bratch must be, though it is not here, for here there is nothing left to do, since all over this world of ours our populations lie dying in their icy homes. Bratch I am not, since Bratch is what I did—and what is my name, Johor, what is my name?"

And Pedug: "Where species reproduce themselves, where the young are born continually to replace those that have to die, there Pedug is, since Pedug has to be. Pedug is re-created always and everywhere, in every time and place, where Pedug is needed. So Pedug is not lost and gone because Pedug no longer exists on our planet. But I am not Pedug, Johor, and—what is my name?"

So it went, with every one of us, and the dark was heavy around us, and the chant, or song, or plaint, continued through the night, one after another of us, asking Johor, asking him, saying where and how and why, but answering ourselves, answering all we wanted to know ourselves, but ending always with that question we could not answer, since it was beyond us—what am I, who am I, and what is my name? Or, *what was our name?*—we, the Representatives, who represented now no skills, or abilities, or working functions, but who still sat there, cold and small and so very few, on that hillside, through the night, all through the night—and then the weak sun was shining dimly, a greyish gleam from greyish skies, and there was no colour left anywhere, for snow had fallen gently and silently, and the tall column Canopus had set there rose up out of fresh soft white, through which pushed the tips of low plants and the stiff dead grasses.

"There is one of us who still has a name," said Alsi, as we became silent, since everyone had spoken.

"But Marl is not here," one said. "The Keepers of the Herds are not here."

"And the herds are not here either, yet there is nowhere else for them to be."

We sat on there, that day, as the snow fell quietly around us, for Johor said nothing, and we did not know what it was we ought to to be doing.

And, as the light went, for another night, three figures came staggering towards us out of the gloom, and fell among us, breathing deep and painfully, and slept for a time, while we waited. These were Marl, and until they spoke, we could not feel that this particular stage of our being together was concluded.

It was in the night that they came up out of their exhaustion, and told us the tale of the herds—yes, it was Doeg we listened to for a while, Marl as Doeg, and this was what we were told.

That multitude of great hungry beasts found themselves crowding closer together every day, as the snows spread down and around them, making a natural corral of snowbanks, a barrier that the beasts showed no disposition to cross, since all the food that remained to them on the entire planet was in this small area around the tall black column. The hay masses from the last summer did not provision them for long, and then they browsed on the wiry plants and the bitter grasses, and then on the soil that is half vegetable. And still the snow crept in around them, and soon they stood together body to body, many thousands of them, a multitude, and there was nothing to eat. Many died, and those that were alive were spurred by their situation into an intelligence no one could have believed possible to them—they pushed the corpses out of the mass of the living with those horns of theirs that were so heavy and, we had thought when we first saw the beasts, so useless: What could they possibly be used for? Yet these horns had turned over the soil, when it became necessary to eat it, had dug roots out of the earth, had overturned boulders in the desperate search for food, had been used, finally, to push their dead out of what remained of the useable space.

And then, for a time, they stood, facing out into the world of snow, all of them, their tails into the centre. And then Marl, watching from the hillsides, anguished at their inability to aid these poor beasts, saw that from every part of the multitude, small groups of them, and then larger and larger numbers, were breaking away. For days Marl watched how the mass that remained at the pole thinned, and still thinned, as the beasts left. But where were they going? There was nowhere for them to go! Yet they went. Lowing and lumbering, pawing the earth as they went, and scarring it with sweeps and scythings of their horns, as if wishing to damage and wound what would no longer supply them with sustenance; screaming out their rage and despair, their eyes red and wild and furious—these herds thundered up and away in every direction from their last grazing grounds, and then their going, which had shaken the earth, was silent, for the deep snows quieted the battering of those multitudes of hooves. The watchers on the hillsides had heard the wild lamenting bellowing of the herds as they rushed up and into the blizzards—and soon none was left around the pole, there was only the black earth that had been horned up, and fouled with masses of droppings, and eaten quite bare. And not one beast, not one. Marl, then, separating, followed the herds up into the thick blizzards, though following them was not easy, since there was no spoor in those heavy snows. But at last, each one of these Representatives reached the populated area, and thought that perhaps the beasts had believed that here there might be food for them, or at least the companionship of people: who could say what there might be in the minds of these doomed animals, or what degrees of hope or intelligence were being forced out of them by their situation? But no, the herds had thundered up to the old towns and villages, empty now, and gone through them, not pausing for anything, except when some beast needed to punish and scar as had been done in the south-lands, their old feeding grounds, and had raked horns into soil—so they directed the thrust of their horns along the sides of buildings and sheds and pens, and trampled down what they could, till the settlements looked as if we had destroyed them as we left. And then the herds had gone on—with nowhere to go. Where the wall had collapsed, making passes into the terrible lands of the perpetual blizzards, the herds had climbed up, and then stood waiting on the other side, white beasts now, their coats heavy with snow, their breath white on white air, till all of their particular group had joined them. Having assembled, as if this had been some plan worked out by them, they all charged up into the north, all to-gether, bellowing and lamenting, to their certain deaths.

Marl, at various places along the wall, where it had fallen for-ward under the glaciers, saw this, saw the herds go off to seek death. And having seen it and understood, met together again, and then, knowing that there was no point at all in following the beasts, for they would have been swallowed up by the blizzards, travelled slowly down to where they knew we all would be. We, the Representa-tives, sitting on our snowy hillside, waiting. Waiting, as it turned out, for them, for Marl, who was no longer Marl, since there were no beasts left alive on our planet anywhere, not one, and so—else-where Marl worked, had to work; in other times and places Marl was and had to be, Marl used the skills of matching and mating and making and feeding and breeding and caring. Marl could not cease to be, since Marl was needed. But here, with us, on our cold planet, Marl was not. "And so, Johor, since we are no longer Marl, what is our name? For while I know I am not what I was, am not Marl, since I was what I did—well, now I do nothing, but here I am, am something, I sit here, among the falling snow, with us all, I look at you, Johor, you look at us, at me—and I feel myself to be here, here; I have thoughts and I have feelings—but where are they, what are they, these thoughts, these feelings, in these packages of frozen bones and chilly flesh? So I am not nothing, Johor, yet what am I? If I have a name, then what is it?"

And so it was with all of us, Johor with the Representatives, sitting there on our cold hillside, while the snow fell, it fell, it fell, so that we sat to our waists in light loose snow, and then the white pall was up to our shoulders—and first one, then another, rose slowly up out of the white as if out of water, shaking flakes and crumbs and clots of snow everywhere, and soon we were all standing, with the white drift up to our mid-thighs, and still the snow fell, it was falling with no signs of any end to it at all. We stood facing in to each other, looking into each other's eyes. There was not one word of Canopus, or of rescues—all that way of thinking seemed to us to belong to some distant childishness; and we could hardly remember, between the lot of us, how we had been in those days of our juvenescence, and now our thoughts were of a very different necessity. Then we turned ourselves so that we all, every one, faced away from the southern extremity of our planet, marked by the slim black shining column which, however, was beginning now to grey over with frost, so that soon it would hardly be visible where it stood amid the heaping drifts and flying clouds of snow. Our faces were to the north, and we began to move in unison, as if there was no other thing that could be done, as if what we had to do was ordained for us, and inevitable—we, like the empty and starving herds before us, were heading up into the realms of the winter; but it was a winter that would soon have covered everything, claimed everything, and our little planet would be swinging there in space, all white and glittering while the sun and the stars shone on it, and then, being all frozen over, with nothing left on it that had been living—what new processes would begin, once the processes of freezing had been accomplished? For nothing can be static and steady and permanent, it could not possibly be that our little world would spin there in space, unaltering, a planet of snow and ice: no, it would go on, gathering more to itself as a snowball does when travelling, or change into something else entirely, become a world we could not begin to imagine, with our senses tuned as they were to Planet 8—and not even this Planet 8, the freezing one, but the old and delightful world of the time before The

Ice . . . no, changes we could not begin to imagine would—must—come to this home of ours, but they would be of no concern to us, for we would not be here.

We moved on, slowly, with our faces to the freezing winds that came down on us, came pitilessly, not ceasing at all, day or night; we went on cold, empty, as insubstantial inside our thick coats as if we were already bones and bits of dried tendon and skin. And Johor was with us, one of us, and his eyes looked back at us, from between the shaggy fringes of his hood, with the same hollow and painful and peering way we all had to use—for the snow glare was in our eyes, and in our minds, and there was no way of shutting it out and finding a soft and companionable darkness where we could rest; for even when the dark did come down, there was so much of the snow-light in us we could not shut our lids, they would not stay shut, but flew open, as if we had the snow and ice inside us as well as out, and our eyes were windows that looked both ways on to landscapes of white, white, a flat hard white.

Half blinded, deaf with the perpetually screaming winds, numbed, dying, we stumbled past the snow huts and sheds we had built for the populations to take refuge in from the advancing glaciers—and did not look inside, for we knew what we would find. As we went through this zone, it was evident that soon the little excrescences of snow and ice, small rounds and bumps among the drifts, would have gone under the white, for already some were gone, quite covered over. And, looking back from the mountain passes that led up into the parts of the planet that had been so thronged with people, we could not see now where these ice settlements were—or had been, for the storms were so thick between us and them. We went on, the few of us, looking out as we went for our old towns, but the glaciers had come down over them, we could not see any sign of settlements or cities, though once we did go struggling past a room sticking up out of the snow, that had square apertures all around, and, in it, some sticks and bits that had been furniture but had been pulverized by the cold. This room was the very top of a tall building, and we were advancing past it at a level where once only the great solitary birds of the age of the cold had swung and circled. And, when we looked ahead of us for something like an escarpment or a cliff, there was nothing at all: the ice pushing down from above the wall had brought it all crashing and crumbling down, and in any case it was now a long way beneath where we travelled over the crests and billows of the snow. So we crossed over that famous wall of ours, the impregnable, the un-breachable, the impervious: the wall that would stand there for-ever between us and disaster, until Canopus would come with her shining fleets. We crossed it without knowing when we did, and were in a landscape where there were no mountains or hills, unless they were of ice or piled snow, for all the natural unevennesses of the terrain had been buried.

It is not true to say that we travelled easily, for we laboured and stumbled and dragged ourselves forward—but this was not because we contended with inclines and descents of mountains and valleys. Yet it was such long hard dragging work. There was nothing left of us! We were as empty as if scoured inside with wind as well as out. We were truly nothing but skin and bone and our poor hearts thumped sluggishly and irregularly, trying to move the thick blood through our drying veins and arteries. We were half dead, and how hard it was, to shift forward these desiccating carcasses even a few steps at a time.

How heavy we were—how very very heavy . . . The drag on every particle of our bodies of the gravity of the spin of the planet was as if we were being held fast by it, and not merely by the thick-nesses of the snow. Heavy, heavy, heavy—was the pull of our mor-tality; even though we were all as transparent as shadows and the flesh on our bones had long since dwindled down and gone. Heavy, the shuffling steps we took, one after another, making ourselves, forcing ourselves to move, our wills hammering there in the pain-ful efforts of our hearts: *Move . . . move . . . move . . . yes, that's it . . . take one more step—yes, that's it . . . and now another . . . yes, and now just one more . . . move . . . and keep moving . . .* and so it was with every one of us, dragging ourselves there, among the clouds of snow that hung so low over the snowdrifts it was hard to tell what was air and what had already fallen from the air. We were half-ghosts, half gone, and yet so heavy we could feel the weight of us depending on the substance of our wills, hanging there, dragging—and what was this thing, *will*, that kept us moving up and on, into the high passes of snow, towards the other pole, the far extremity of our planet? In and through and among these bundles of bones and skin and already desiccated tissues, burned something else, *will*—and where was it, that pulse or pull in the vast spaces that lie between the minute pull or pulses that make up the atom?

Heavy, heavy, oh so heavy, we dragged and pushed ourselves; we waded and seemed to swim, up and up and through, and at nights we rested together, poor wraiths, while the winds shrieked or the stars talked overhead. When we reached where we knew must be the gorge where Nonni had slipped, there was a clear fresh sweep of white, and the caves we had sheltered in were buried and gone; and when we came to the high valley between the ringing peaks where we had crouched to stare at the glitter of the stars and heard them rustle and sing, what we saw were the little tips of the mountains, hillocks merely, and if we had not known mountains were there, could not have guessed that they stood so tall and sharp. We made a stop there, as dark fell, in a hollow at the top of one of the small hills; and the winds rose screaming and we felt the snow thud and push and whirl all around us—and in the morning there was the most marvellous sight. For we were huddled between rocks on the summit of a great mountain—the winds had in the night cleared the valley of loose snow, so that we saw it as we had on our previous visit here, emptied. The winds had a pattern and a movement that filled this valley to the top, and then swept it: all over the planet the snow masses were moved about, piled high and then blasted away again, heaped up and then whisked off by gales to be dumped somewhere else. We looked down at a glassy glittering icy place many days walking across and very deep, between enormous icy black peaks. All we looked at had a glassy awfulness that hurt into our dying eyes; and as we peered down over the edge of the miniature valley we were stranded in at the top of the mountain peak, we knew we would never leave it. How could we, weak as we were, descend the ghastly precipices of that peak? And so, for the last time with our old eyes, we sat close and looked into each other's faces, until, one after another, our faces shuttered themselves in death, and our bundles of bones settled

inside the heaps of our shag-skin coats, so that, as we slid away from
that scene, and saw it with eyes we had not known we possessed,
all we could see was what looked like a herd of beasts crouched
in sleep or in death high up there on a mountaintop.

We went on together, light now, so buoyant and easy in moving
that it was with disbelief and with horror we thought back to our
so recent dreadful heaviness, the old weight of us, each step or lurch
forward against the pull and the drag that held every tiniest atom
in a lock. Our new eyes had no steady perspective. We went floating
onwards, free and light, and when we looked back for orientation at
the carcasses we had inhabited, we saw only that we were among
throngs of the most marvellous intricate structures and shapes:
glittering crystals surrounded us, all different, each a marvel of sub-
tlety and balance, each a thing we could have stayed to contemplate
and wonder over . . . yet there were myriads of them, they came
floating and drifting all about us, and, as our eyes kept changing
their capacity, sometimes these crystals seemed enormous, as large
as we were, and sometimes small. It was not at once that we understood that these multitudes of infinitely various shapes were snowflakes; that were, or had recently been, our enemy: it was by the
agency of such loveliness that our little planet had slowly been done
to death. But we had not suspected it, had not known when we
stretched out a hand to let a white flake settle there, so that we
might show it to our children: "See? That is snow! That is the water
vapour that is always in the air around us in a new shape"—had
never thought that this little crumb, or froth of white, might be
seen thus, as a conglomeration of structures so remarkable that one
might examine them with admiration that could never wear out.
Floating through them, feeling ourselves to change shape and size
constantly, we tried to stay our movement, so that we could take
our fill of gazing at these miracles; but that scene dissolved and
went, the crystal structures vanished, for they belonged to some
sphere or realm that we had passed through. Now, when we looked
back to that huddle of bodies under their piles of dirty skins, to
see how far we had travelled from that mountain peak, we saw them
as webs and veils of light, saw the frail lattice of the atomic structure, saw the vast spaces that had been what in fact we mostly

were—though we had not had eyes to comprehend that, even if
our minds knew the truth. But the little dazzle or dance we looked
at, the fabric of the atomic structure, dissolved as we watched: yes,
we saw how those old bodies of ours inside their loads of hide were
losing their shapes, how the atoms and the molecules were losing
their associations with each other, and were melding with the substance of the mountain. Yes, what we were seeing now with our
new eyes was that all the planet had become a fine frail web or
lattice, with the spaces held there between the patterns of the atoms.
But what new eyes were these that could see our old home thus, as
interlocking structures of atoms, and where were we, the Representatives?—what were we, and how did we seem to those who
could watch us, with their keener finer sight? For, certainly, as we
changed eyes and ways of seeing so that every moment it seemed
that we inhabited a different world, or zone, or reality, it must be
that others could watch us, see us—but see what? If we had lost our
old shapes, which had already disintegrated and gone into the substance of mountain and snow and wind and rock, lost those faint
webs or veils or templates that had been more space than substance
—if we had lost what we had been, then we were still something,
and moved on together, a group of individuals, yet a unity, and had
to be, must be, patterns of matter, matter of a kind, since everything is—webs of matter or substance or something tangible, though
sliding and intermingling and always becoming smaller and smaller
—matter, a substance, for we were recognising ourselves as existent;
we were feelings, and thought, and will. These were the web and
the woof and the warp of our new being, though in our old being
there had seemed no home or place for them, and we had imagined
how love and hate and the rest had howled and swept and pulsed
about in the vast spaces that lie between the core of an atom (if
anything that dissolves as you think of it may be termed a core)
and the particles that surround it (if a vibration and a flow may
be called a particle)—and these feelings and thoughts made up our
new selves, or self, and our minds were telling us that we were
still a tenuous though strict dance, just as our old minds had told
us what we were, though we had not had eyes to see what we were.
Once, before we became dead beasts lying frozen on a mountain-

top, these layers or veils fitted into each other, had been a whole, had functioned together—but now one pattern had already sunk back into the physical substance of Planet 8, and another went forward, our eyes changing with every moment so that we were continually part of a new scene, or time. Nor were we something already fixed, with an entity that could not be changed, for we came upon a ghost or a feeling or a flavour that we named *Nonni*: a faintly glittering creature or shape or dance that had been, we knew, Nonni, the dead boy, Alsi's companion, and this entity or being came to us, and married with us, with our new substance, and we all went on as one, but separate, in our journey towards the pole.

Who went? And what was our name?

The teacher of children was there; and the guardian of the waters; the maker and creator of grains and fruits and plants; the keeper and breeder of animals; the storyteller who continually makes and re-makes the memories of populations; the tender of the very small and vulnerable; the healer—the discoverer of medicines and remedies; the traveller who visits planets so that knowledge may not be imprisoned and unshared—all these were there, among us and of us; all our functions and the capacities of our work were in the substance of these new beings, this Being, we now were—Johor with and of us, Johor mingled with us, the Representative of Canopus part of the Representative of Planet 8, the destroyed one— destroyed at least for our purposes—for who could say how this lump of ice spinning in the spaces of the heavens would modify itself, becoming gas perhaps, on its way back to soil and a shape and substance that would be recognisable to the eyes we once had owned.

The Representative swept on and up, like a shoal of fishes or a flock of birds; one, but a conglomerate of individuals—each with its little thoughts and feelings, but these shared with the others, tides of thought, of feeling, moving in and out and around, making the several one.

What were we seeing there, feeling there—and where? In what place or time were we, then: what were we, and when? We did not see wastes of snow or ice, no, but a perpetual shifting and changing—we were seeing our planet in a myriad guises, or possibilities.

We saw it in a flash or a glimpse as it had been, our warm and lovely place where everything had blessed us, and beside this brief vision, a thousand variations of the same, each slightly different, so that each one, had we seen it by itself, could have been judged by us as a stage in the development of our planet—but seen thus, merging so fast, and so subtly different, we knew that what we saw were *possibilities*, what could have been, but had not been, not in our space and time. But had been elsewhere? Yes, that was it, we were observing how, behind or beside or beyond—at any rate, some *where* or *when*—the various stages of development of our planet, had been so many others, the possibilities that had not been given actuality in the level of existence we had known, had experienced; but hovered just behind the veil, potentials, what might have been or could have been . . . Myriads there were, the unachieved possibilities; but each real and functioning on its own level—*where* and *when* and *how?*—each world every bit as valid and valuable as what we had known as real. Just as once, I, Doeg, had stood in front of mirrors in my old self and seen stretching out in an interminable line of possibilities, all the variations in the genetic storehouse made visible—sometimes so similar to what I was that I could hardly tell the difference, but then more and more of me, each a variation, and a variation farther away from what "I" was—each one the possible and potential housing of this feeling of me, Doeg, some easily recognisable to my fellows as I, Doeg, and others so wildly distant that only a turn of the head or the slightest familiarity in a slide of the eyes or a set of the shoulders could say, "Yes, this, too, is of the family of Doeg, is Doeg's potential that did not step forward into this dimension or place"—so now we could see all the worlds that were not our planet, but lay there, lapping and touching it, each an absolute and a reality in its place and time.

Oh who then were Doeg and Alsi—were Klin and Nonni and Marl and the rest of us? What was our planet, which was one of so many? And, as we swept on there, ghosts among the ghostly worlds, we felt beside us, and in us, and with us, the frozen and dead populations that lay buried under the snows. Inside caves and huts and mounds of ice and snow the peoples of our old world lay frozen—the carcasses of these were held there for as long as the ice stayed, before it changed, as everything must, to something else—a swirl of gases perhaps, or seas of leaping soil, or fire that had to burn until it, too, changed . . . *must* change . . . *must* become something else. But what these had been, our peoples, our *selves*— were with us then, *were* us, had become us—could not be anything but us, their representatives—and we, together, the Representative, at last found the pole that was the extremity of our old planet, the dark cold pole that had been built, once, to guide in the space-fleets of Canopus, when they visited us. There we left that planet, and came to where we are now. We, the Representative, many and one, came here, where Canopus tends and guards and instructs.

You ask us how the Canopean Agents seemed to us in the days of The Ice.

This tale is our answer.

Afterword

A foreword on these lines almost got itself put in front of the third volume in this series, *The Sirian Experiments*, which novel came to be written as a direct result of nearly fifty years of being fascinated by the two British expeditions to the Antarctic led by Robert Falcon Scott, the first in 1901–4, the second in 1910–13. No, it is not snow and ice as such, but rather some social processes of that time and of this, so strongly illuminated by the expeditions, that interest me. But I knew that more casual, or literal-minded, readers would not easily see how *The Sirian Experiments* could result from preoccupation with polar exploration, and so I let the intention slide. And then the next novel, this one, turned out to be so wintry that no difficulty could be found in making the equation: a long immersion in polar exploration and a novel about a planet freezing to death. Yet people with an understanding of the creative—or, on the electrical analogy, the transforming—processes would expect just as readily a novel about deserts or about any extreme of climate or geography or behaviour. This afterword, then, should be considered as belonging to both *The Sirian Experiments* and *The Making of the Representative for Planet 8*, though more to the first than to the second.

There is a practical reason why it is a good thing the afterword is in the back of the short book, though it was not planned. When I told the English publisher this fourth volume would be very short, he was pleased, and not only because this would mean less trees, paper, printers' work, ink, bindings, but because in this country there is a bias in favour of short books, much more likely to be good ones, and of real quality, than long ones, and this in spite of Dickens and all those wordy and indubitably first-rate Victorians.

The extracts on pages 135 and 137 are from Apsley Cherry-Garrard's *The Worst Journey in the World* (London: Chatto & Windus, 1913). Those on pages 141, 142, 143, and 144 (top) are from George Seaver's *Edward Wilson of the Antarctic: Naturalist and Friend* (London: John Murray, 1933).

Whereas, when I said to my American publisher that it was so short, he said at once, mocking himself and his nation, but meaning it, in the way they have over there, "But you *know* that we can take only big books seriously." So over there (or over here, according to how you look at it) big *is* beautiful, after all.

There is in Cambridge a building devoted to the records of the Antarctic expeditions, but I have not been there. Mine is not a systematic study, but the other kind where, knowing that you must have affinities with a subject or a theme because of the way it keeps appearing in your life, but always differently aspected, the way a landscape looks different from different parts of a mountain, you wait for things to happen: a book you didn't know existed found on a library shelf; a chance meeting with a relative of one of the explorers; a letter in a newspaper; or a friend, knowing of your interest, sends a biography seen on a secondhand book stall in Brighton. This way of studying means you may be unaware of facts known to even apprentice researchers, but if you keep facts and possibilities floating about in your head, they can combine in unexpected ways.

I first heard of Scott and his band of heroes thus. It was in the middle of Africa, in the old Southern Rhodesia, now Zimbabwe, on my father's farm. We, the family, were in the habit of sitting outside the house in the open, to enjoy the daytime or nighttime skies, and the weather, and the view which was miles in every direction, a wild and mostly empty landscape ringed by mountains. The point is, we were hundreds of miles from the sea, and England was a long way off, and so in time were the Scott expeditions. It was nearly always hot, and the skies spectacular, either wonderfully blue and empty or full of the energetic cloud movement made by heat rising off sun-cooked earth and vegetation. Through the dry months forest fires were usually burning somewhere close. There, most vividly in my memory, is my mother, standing head back, hands out, in a posture of dramatic identification. I do not remember if there was an amazing sunset, but there should have been one, or at least a storm. My mother, choked with emotion, and radiant, for she enjoyed these moments, is saying: "And when I think of Captain Oates going off alone to die in the blizzards—oh, he *was* a most gallant gentleman!" And I then, with the raucous bray of the adolescent: "But what else could he have done? And anyway, they were all in the dying business." I regret the bray, but not the sentiment; in fact it seems to me that I was as clear-sighted then as I have been since, and I envy the way that hard girl bulldozed her way through pieties and humbug, for there is no doubt life softens you up: tolerance makes nougat of us all. My father was not sentimental and, as always during my mother's high moments, was uncomfortable; and certainly said something like: "Oh, come off it, old girl," and, to me: "Yes, I dare say, but do you have to be uncompromising about everything?" Yes, I did, and the reasons I did are not unconnected with the subject of these remarks.

Not that my father was indifferent to Scott and the rest, for these were English achievements, and, as with my mother, to be English, it went without saying, was to be the best.

It is hard now to understand what *England* meant to my parents, who were of the same generation as those heroic explorers. A word can be a powerful drug for one generation, and as bland as milk for the next. It is not irrelevant to this theme either that foreign readers, and this includes for the moment Americans, will have little idea about Scott the explorer, any more than have most people in Britain under the age of let's say forty. Blank looks are what I get when I blow that old trumpet: "Scott of the Antarctic!" They say, "Scott? Didn't he discover the South Pole?" Yet, so short a time ago, Scott, the Antarctic, the names of the men who worked with him, made up one of those myths or pieties that every nation has to have as inspirational fuel. There was this band of dedicated demigods, gallant gentlemen one and all, and anyone who might dare to hint at the possibility of flaws would have been beaten up. As bad as suggesting, for instance, that there were ordinary human beings on The Long March . . . but supply your own national pieties, stick in this empty space the faces of your own heroes.

It was Bernard Shaw who said something like this: that heroes were never in short supply, that people always rushed forward to die for causes, good and bad, but that we could do with less heroism, and more hard thinking. On subjects of this sort Shaw can usually be found to have said it already.

Recently, in Britain, there is a different mood about Scott, suggesting that a reassessment of him as leader and of his management of the 1910–13 expedition is about to surface. There are signs that he is about to become something not far from a villain. It is possible he was less than always competent, and he made mistakes: this is not a question of his having made the kind of mistakes everyone does make, but the kind that no even ordinarily able leader should make. In short, we are in the process of swinging from one extreme to another, and I don't want to be part of that: I am interested in the way this kind of reassessment happens, and the timing of it. What lies behind facts like these: that so recently one could not have said Scott was not perfect without earning at least sorrowful disapproval; that a year after the Gang of Four were perfect, they were villains; that in the fifties in the United States a nothing-man called McCarthy was able to intimidate and terrorise sane and sensible people, but that in the sixties young people summoned before similar committees simply laughed. No, those young Americans should not have imagined that had *they* been summoned before the earlier committees they would have laughed, for they would not have: they were as good as their parents, but no better: something had happened in the meantime, the *atmosphere had changed,* as we say, using one of the phrases that is an excuse for not thinking. I could fill pages, volumes, with facts illustrating this theme, that the heresies of one year are the pieties of the next, and vice versa, and so can everyone past the age of indiscriminate enthusiasms—and so could anyone at all, if he wanted to. But for some reason we cannot apply the obvious lessons of history to ourselves.

Why? Is it possible that we could learn not to impose on each other these sacred necessities, in the name of some dogma or other, with results that inevitably within a decade will be dismissed with: We made mistakes. It is only too easy to imagine The Spirit of History (we have had so much practice at it!), a blowzy but complacent female, wearing the mask of the relevant ruler or satrap: "Dearie me!" she smiles, "but I have made a mistake again!" And into the dustbin go holocausts, famines, wars, and the occupants of a million prisons and torture chambers.

I have lived through several of these dramatic changes; there are obviously, and very soon, more to come. Private and ironic thoughts on the subject are one of the consolations of growing old. What happens must be something like the slow adding of grain to grain on one side of a pair of scales, though you can't see this, only deduce it. And then a sudden reversal of the balance. Surely these are processes we can learn to study, particularly when they recur so often, and when they seem to be speeding up, like everything else?

For instance. I was one of the handful of people who in the early fifties tried to get journalists, members of parliament, politicians, to see that things were not well in southern Africa. To say we were talking about criminally oppressive tyrannies was then not possible; no, it had to be wrapped up. Even so we were treated with tolerant amusement . . . dismissed as wrong-headed . . . red . . . anti-British . . . crazy. Inside ten years the idea that what was going on in southern Africa—in South Africa and Southern Rhodesia—should at the very least be examined, was a respectable view. Was "received opinion." Ten years later—but by then it was too late. Of course. I say "of course" as shorthand for my suspicion that this is a law at work. It would have been the easiest thing in the world to prevent that war, if common sense had had anything to do with it—but when does common sense have anything to do with it? If the whites had had the ability to look coolly for five minutes at analogous historical processes—but when, ever, has a ruling caste had this capacity?

No, this is not "We told you so!" This is for the braying adolescent. After "I told you so" comes the anger at the waste of it all, the stupidity, the preventability neglected . . . but what if it is always like this? Has to be like this? Is there is a law at work? For then there is no point in all these emotions, they are a waste of time, the sick anger as well as *I told you so*: what we need is to think, and not emote. Politicians and rulers are not the makers of events, but their puppets: well, then, one should not expect anything else. But it seems that the repetitiveness of historical, of sociological processes is not even noticed. Now, as young people come into their inheritance, to choose one or other of the fifty-seven varieties of socialism, they all, without ado or effort, opine that there is a tyranny, white over black, down there at the bottom of Africa.

But suppose their counterparts had known it in good time? And—but here is the point—while they are accepting, just as their predecessors did, "received opinion," what nascent ideas are they ignoring? Ideas which, when it is too late, will be easily adopted by their kind in twenty years—ideas which will then have lost their energy, will have become worn out?

I used to think that the sequence—futile and derided or punished warnings by the few, then these warnings slowly being accepted to form the basis of a new attitude, which by that time is already out of date—was peculiar to politics and to religious movements with a mass basis. But you can see the processes at work in every sphere from sport to literature.

And, for that matter, in yourself.

In the political sphere, the ruling strata of a country, a state, are identified with their own propaganda . . . no, they don't use it, for that to my mind is one of the formulas of Marxist rhetoric which are substitutes for thought; they are used by it, for they are identified with their own justifications for being in power, always self-deceiving ones. When has any ruler said "I am a wicked tyrant"? The Shah of Iran and Amin of Uganda thought well of themselves. It is inevitable that when faced with facts demonstrating that such and such a colonised country, or less favoured part of their own country, or town, or district is suffering hardship, lack of freedom, tyranny, then these people will always and invariably deny the facts. Nothing else can be expected. I remember that when I was going through the business of having a house compulsorily purchased by the Greater London Council, I was enabled to observe the bullying, the sharp-dealing, the sheer corruption of the council employees, when dealing with the unfortunate people not middle-class, not able to stand up for themselves. I went to various acquaintances who were town councillors or otherwise engaged in the processes of public management; but no, the familiar tolerant smile, the hidden impatience: such awfulness could not possibly be going on, not under *their* benevolent aegis.

One may formulate a rule, tentatively, thus: People in power, people at the top of an institution or department or ministry, never allow themselves to know what is being done by their subordinates, for that would mean losing their image of themselves as the only persons fit to be in charge, in power. (Let alone losing their jobs.) I simply cannot believe that the world has always been so stupidly mismanaged as it is now, that the poor have always been so helpless and so disregarded by the people at the top. There have been nations, states, communities, in the past when the rulers made it their business to know what went on in the lower reaches of their administrations. In certain kingdoms in our Middle Ages, in the Middle East, rulers appointed officials to go about incognito, or even went themselves, testing out this or that official's behaviour. But such is the degree of cynicism we have fallen into, it is hard to believe that if we tried out something of the sort ourselves, the investigators would not almost at once become the creatures of the officials whose behaviour they were testing.

But what interests me is that this idea has gone from among those we consider useful as means to good government. At what point did it lose its force . . . become a quaint relic . . . a symptom of personal despotism? When will it return again, and under what kind of regime? I think there must be definite lifespans for ideas or sets of related ideas. They are born (or reborn), come to maturity, decay, die, are replaced. If we do not at least ask ourselves if this is in fact a process, if we do not make the attempt to treat the mechanisms of ideas as something we may study, with impartiality, what hope have we of controlling them?

No, I have not digressed: this kind of speculation is what gets provoked by studying that extraordinary series of events, the exploration of the Antarctic, or—to use our imperial way of putting it—the discovery of the South Pole, a prize which brought the cry out of Scott: "Great God! This is an awful place!" So awful is it there are not even any animals: nothing was there before people, though a bird perhaps sometimes went past. And so the South Pole has at least the distinction of having been really discovered, unlike, let's say, the Victoria Falls or the Niagara Falls, known by Africans and by Indians for at least hundreds of years before being "discovered" by the whites. (This observation has of course a tired and banal flavour, but until quite recently was abrasive.)

In the decades before the First World War most of the European nations explored the Antarctic, the different teams competing, a display on a vast stage, illuminated as it were by that new toy, the popular newspapers; and it does rather seem now as if "the eyes of the world" were more on that drama than on the incidents that were building up toward the war. Which is a fact not without interest in itself. The two aspects of national rivalry, in full view; and to the Europeans, nothing could have seemed more normal. But this is how it all looked to quite a lot of people not European: there was little Europe, strutting and bossing up there in its little corner, like a pack of schoolboys fighting over a cake.

There are people who believe that when our successors look back at our time, nationalism will seem as lethally stupid as religious wars seem to most of us. And even in the ugly climate we live in, the International Geophysical Year 1958 was possible, which was partly the result of the best aspects of the rivalry and the aspirations of the explorers themselves. For, just as in the trenches the fighting soldiers kept decency and common sense about their opponents and it was the civilians who raved and hated, so, in this matter of polar exploration, the men actually doing the work left the worst envies and jealousies to the onlookers.

Right at the end, it was Norway and Britain who were left as rivals. The Norwegian team was headed by Roald Amundsen, and the British team by Scott.

Amundsen got to the South Pole first by about a month. And he got safely home again, without loss of life. The British team lost lives and suffered all kinds of mishaps. The reasons for one team doing so well, and the other not, have been analysed ever since. One was that Amundsen was supported by his government, and the British team shamefully neglected. This kind of niggardly short-sightedness seems for some reason a perennial characteristic of British government. At any rate Scott, a sensitive man, had to go running around cap in hand begging for money, and it wasn't good for him. They couldn't afford to buy and equip a proper ship, whereas Amundsen's was built for the ice. The British expedition was a scientific one, whereas the Norwegian had only one aim, to get to the Pole and back. The Norwegians had every kind of experience necessary, but the British did not know nearly so much about snow and ice and the handling of dogs. But these comparisons, which one could multiply, are perhaps off the point.

For what has to strike you, as soon as you start to read the diaries, the letters, the records, is a difference in tone, in atmosphere.

Amundsen's book describes in a sensible non-boastful way a sensible and efficient expedition. It is quiet in tone, and practical.

Now you turn to the records of the Scott expedition (1910–13), and at once you are in a different world.

Atmosphere, this word we use so easily, what is it? A journalist will ask, or a researcher: What happened then, or there? Who said that, and why? What is your version of what went on? . . . And you sit there, remembering all kinds of incidents, telling the truth as far as you can; and then you see it is all no use. For there is nothing you can do to convey an atmosphere, a *Zeitgeist*. You can offer incidents to illustrate that lost time (which may be a very short time ago indeed), but more often than not they seem bizarre and the people involved lunatic. You find yourself saying desperately: You see, the atmosphere has changed so much that . . .

It is exactly the same as when you are telling a friend a dream. You describe a series of incidents, like the plot of a film. I was in that place and I said this, and then . . . But the same series of incidents, involving the same people, can be a different dream. It is the atmosphere that is the point. And how to convey that? Feebly you say: The dream had such a strong flavour, it was so compelling, don't you see? Really, it was like . . . but what shall I say? It had a quite unmistakable flavour or taste, and whenever I find myself in a dream with that atmosphere, then I know that . . .

And that is the end of it. No communication possible, unless someone else had the same dream, and that you have to take on trust. In waking life, of course, people did have the same dream, quite unarguably, went through the same events, *experienced the same atmosphere*; so when you say, *Do you remember?* indeed they do, you both do, and you may well exchange a smile that says how impossible it would be to explain that atmosphere to someone who did not live through it.

The records of the two expeditions, Norwegian and British, are of two different emotional events, from different climates of experience. Hard to believe they took place at the same time, in the same place, and with ostensibly more or less the same goals, equipped with men of the same type, many of them known widely as professional explorers, men who knew each other or of each other, and who respected each other's achievements.

But, first, those aspects of the British expedition which at the time were not noticed or questioned at all; for I believe those biases that are the result of the unconscious assumptions of a time are precisely those which people later on marvel at most.

The national biases are still with us, though they are modified, or have shifted ground.

There were no women on the expeditions. At that time the women who were demanding rights were being beaten by policemen, forcibly fed in prisons, derided and jeered at by fine gentlemen, generally ill-treated and often enough by other women. It was simply not possible for women to be on the expeditions. Nor is it a question of blaming anyone, for the idea would not have surfaced. Yet I wonder how many girls lay awake at night, fiercely resentful of the bondage of gentility, their enforced "weakness," thinking: "If only I was there, I'd show them." "I know I could be as brave and resourceful as they are!" "Oh, the bitter tears of unused and patronised and frustrated women!" These are quotations from letters between women, just before the First World War.

Yet women had contributed to nineteenth-century exploration. There were women at work then. There was Isabella Bird, for one.

Behind these dramas of the polar expeditions is a frieze or backdrop of women—no, ladies—who stood elegantly about in their drooping fettering garments, smiling wistfully at these warriors of theirs—and for the most part this is a silent cloud of witnesses. They saw their men off from ports in England, and travelled to New Zealand to take part in farewells, and welcoming ceremonies, and official dinners, and they received reams of letters, and were loved in the reverential, grateful, worshipping way that was how these things went on, then.

There is, to say the least, evidence that they did not always see things as their men did.

As for the wives of other ranks, they said even less.

Which brings us to the class divisions, so rigid, that you read saying Oh no, it really is *not* possible. Yet they were taken for granted. Were basic. Were right. Natural. Good for discipline. Were, one cannot help suspecting, something to do with God, virtue, the divine order and, most certainly, the divinely ordained greatness of England. (It was always *England* these men apostrophized, not Britain, a compromised and adulterated word, and idea.)

There were officers and there were men, and they had separate eating and sleeping places, even in the most extreme situations; and the names of the officers were known to every man, woman and child throughout the British nation, while those of the men were less known though they did the same dangerous and difficult work. Even when six men were holed up for a long Antarctic winter, in an ice cave, with every possibility they would all soon die of cold and starvation, the class divisions were rigidly kept, with the concurrence of both sides that this was the only possible way to do things: officers lay on one side, and men on the other, and they all supported each other with the tenderest solicitude.

It was the influence of the British navy, of Scott, that was the source of the inflexibility over class: there were those, Shackleton among them, who thought it ridiculous. But the navy surely had nothing to do with this pervasive mood or style of the 1910–13 expedition, so fervent, so exalted, for the British team were engaged in some very high enterprise, a desperate, dangerous, life-and-death business . . . but at once it will be objected that Amundsen's effort was just as dangerous and heroic. Very true: just because he succeeded so magnificently, it doesn't mean he couldn't easily have died with all of his team. He took chances, as he said himself— diced with death, as they say. But no one died, and there is nothing in what Amundsen wrote that suggests he expected to die.

That the British were not supported by their government, that their ship was so inadequate and dangerous, that there was so much suffering because of it, certainly contributed to the emotional note: we against the world, we this small band of brothers doing our duty against such odds!

Yes, there is a danger, writing about that time which is so unlike ours, of misinterpretation. For instance, this word *duty*. Their devotion to their tasks and responsibilities was total, because of their attitude to duty. To us now (1980), it is an absurd word, and few of us would dream of putting an ounce more effort into anything than we have to. On the contrary, people who lie, cheat, and get away with it are admired rather than not. In those days children were taught to be responsible, honourable, reliable, and the men on those expeditions judged each other and themselves by these standards. But the 1910–13 expedition particularly was distinguished by lofty exalted emotionalism; and though it was linked with duty to England, God, science, and their best selves, surely it was all beyond what was necessary?

It seems to me that everything they did has to be seen in this other light: they were engaged, or the key people were, particularly Wilson, and some consciously, in an attempt to transcend themselves. This was the real driving force of the expedition from the very first, and before all the setbacks and difficulties, the neglect by government, the mishaps and the mistakes that gave the emotional impetus. But probably if the expedition had gone well things would not have been so different, given the natures of the men involved. This need to break out of our ordinary possibilities—the cage we live in that is made of our habits, upbringing, circumstances, and which shows itself so small and tight and tyrannical when we do try to break out—this need may well be the deepest one we have? At any rate, it can be observed all the time and everywhere. (And probably accounts for the enthusiasm with which people throw themselves into wars, but that is a subject outside my scope here.) Every one of us thinks wistfully of the times when we were able to go without sleep for days, work so far beyond our ordinary capacity we don't know how we did it, perform what seem to our pedestrian selves as miraculously airy feats.

There was the affair of the King Emperor Penguin eggs. Edward Wilson, doctor, biologist, artist, explorer, writer, wanted to obtain some of those eggs, partly because an object of the expedition was to get specimens of bird, animal, and fish life, partly because it was believed that the study of the embryos of the birds would throw light on evolution.

These penguins hatch their eggs in the middle of the Antarctic winter, in the cold black dark, and in inaccessible places. The men had already been working at their limits for months. They were overstrained and overtaxed and, clearly, overwrought. To go off in search of these eggs was folly. Scott thought so, and tried to dissuade Wilson. Wilson himself, once they were on their way, thought so, was anguished because of what he had brought the others into: but of course it was not in the spirit of the thing that they should turn back. The other two men were "Birdie" Bowers, a man of such moral and physical qualities that he stands out, even among those others who were so well equipped with them, and a young man of twenty-four, Apsley Cherry-Garrard, who later wrote the best book about the expedition. Here is a quotation:

> We travelled for Science. Those three small embryos from Cape Crozier, that weight of fossils from Buckley Island, and that mass of material, less spectacular, but gathered just as carefully hour by hour in wind and drift, darkness and cold, were striven for in order that the world may have a little more knowledge, that it may build on what it knows instead of on what it thinks.

The book is *The Worst Journey in the World*, and the chapter called "The Winter Journey" is about the getting of the eggs. The last chapter, called "Never Again," has a startled, bleak feel to it, though it was clearly written in high emotion, and analyses his conclusions about the expedition as a whole. But even then, ten years afterwards, writing with bitter hindsight, the rhetorical glory-making spirit of the expedition breaks through thus, in a passage of common sense about future polar exploration:

> I hope that by the time Scott comes home—for he is coming home: the Barrier is moving, and not a trace of our funeral cairn was found by Shackleton's men in 1916—the hardships that wasted his life will be only a horror of the past, and his via dolorosa a highway as practicable as Piccadilly.

This means, apparently, that in some mystic way the ice and snows of the Antarctic will bear Scott's body back *home*, triumphantly to

England; and if it is being objected that this is the merest rubbishy nonsense, you are wrong: you see, you are leaving the *atmosphere* of the time out of account.

But, the Winter Journey . . . it was very cold, and it was very dark. It is not possible to understand what it was like, for you can say so-and-so below zero, and understand nothing even if you have experienced such temperatures—for almost certainly you were well fed and well clothed and anyway only out for a moment or two. It could take them four hours in the "morning" to ease their frozen selves out of their frozen or sodden sleeping bags and to get their limbs working. They reached the point where they didn't care if they fell into crevasses. When they got back to base, their clothes had to be hacked off them, in chunks. Or there is a glimpse of them on a deadly cold but still night, since for once there were no blizzards or winds, the three of them bent stiffly over, their bodies chattering—"When your body chatters, you can say it is cold . . ."—*with a candle*, trudging miles through the awful snow to bring a sledge—the sledges had to be fetched in relays.

It took six weeks, this impossible journey. They were nearly killed. It was luck, that they survived. When they reached their destination, they had to climb down dangerous cliffs of ice, in pitch-darkness of course, with frostbitten fingers, to reach penguin level, but found their way blocked by walls of ice, and had to worm themselves through and almost could not get back. And then there was a blizzard worse than they imagined was possible, and their tent blew away and . . . everything bad that could happen, happened. During all this Wilson wrote in his diary, taking his gloves off for a few seconds at a time to do it, and Bowers made his meteorological observations, and the three of them loved each other, absolutely, and were ready to die for each other, which of course they were in fact doing, since if they had not got back, their interdependence, their trust, would have amounted to that. I read this part of the book expostulating "No, really, stop it! This is crazy, this is insane, what are you doing it for?" What? Well, to get embryos for the Natural History Museum, and for the glory of England. But what were they really doing? Now that is a very different thing! What comes from these wonderful, appalling pages is the distillate of the spirit of the whole expedition.

When they got their eggs back to England and to the Natural History Museum, of course some stupid official could not be bothered with them, or with the eggs; did not know who they were. But this script was still being written by an artist who knew how it should be: to have these heroic madmen actually welcomed, the eggs taken in the trembling awe they merited—no, too much of an anticlimax. And the first of the scientists to examine the eggs missed an essential point, so one could say that the enterprise had been wasted. If you look at it from that point of view. Which was not Cherry-Garrard's: here is the last paragraph, the summing up.

> And I tell you, if you have the desire for knowledge and the power to give it physical expression, go out and explore. If you are a brave man you will do nothing: if you are fearful you may do much, for none but cowards have need to prove their bravery. Some will tell you that you are mad, and nearly all will say, "What is the use?" For we are a nation of shopkeepers, and no shopkeeper will look at research which does not promise him a financial return within a year. And so you will sledge nearly alone, but those with whom you sledge will not be shopkeepers: that is worth a good deal. If you march your Winter Journeys you will have your reward, so long as all you want is a penguin's egg.

Notice here too the fine gentlemanly scorn for commerce, a spirit which is by no means dead with us.

The Winter Journey was only one of the impossible heroisms bred by the spirit of the expedition.

Here is another. Six men, officers and other ranks, were on a scientific trip, to collect specimens and observe conditions, intending to meet the ship, which was due to pick them up as soon as the ice made it possible. But such were the conditions that it was on the cards the ship would not get through and they would not be picked up. I repeat that they were quite aware of the possibilities. Yet they failed to equip themselves properly. No ship: and they were then faced with surviving until the next Antarctic spring without suitable clothing, or food, or equipment. They dug a hole under the snow, described by a later expedition as a dog kennel. They killed some seals and some penguins. They put themselves into the hole, and kept burning a small stove, fed by seal oil, which filled the cave and blackened the walls and them with greasy smoke. Officers on one side, men on the other, united by loving concern, they lay in their filthy and inadequate sleeping bags, singing songs of a religious and patriotic sort, and talking about England and food. There was, of course, only blubber and penguin to eat, and not much of that. To get their water to boil took an hour or so. They had diarrhoea. They were not however discouraged, and kept themselves going for six months through the Antarctic night by the most intelligent and determined discipline. When the ordeal was over—and when they had gone into the ice cave it was after four months of exhausting exposure and under-feeding—they made a dangerous way back to base, where they were greeted with the news of the deaths of Scott's party. These greasily black, half-starved ghosts then at once volunteered for duty, and went back to work.

It was all like that. There was the business, for instance, of how Scott allowed, at the last minute on an impulse, "Birdie" Bowers to go along with the team of four men who had been chosen to go to the Pole, although they had skis and he had not. It is no business of leaders to make impulsive decisions of this kind, and Scott has been, is being, criticised for it; and indeed it all makes no sense, unless you put yourself, or try to, in that mood of passionate endeavour. "Birdie" Bowers was being given the coveted privilege of being one of those who would actually discover the Pole (which, when they got there, they would find had already been discovered by Amundsen). And when they all lay dying in their tent, I am sure the last thing any of them thought was that it might have been ill advised to allow this last man along, when he was ill equipped: or that it might later be considered a waste to risk an extraordinary man.

No, they lay in their tent dying, the gallant Captain Oates having staggered forth into the blizzards—though the suggestion is that he might very well have decided to do this before (yet what difference would it have made if he had?)—and they were all sustained by knowing that they had done their duty as well as they could, and that they might, had luck been with them, have made it back to base. Actually, it was later decided, they died of simple starvation, for knowledge about what men doing such very heavy work needed in the way of calories was lacking then.

It was not all their fault. Yet Amundsen did not suffer from semistarvation. His team ate dogs all the way to the Pole and back. The Britishers thought ill of them for this, though they ate their horses when necessary.

These were all very intelligent men, some with experience on other expeditions, not all of them polar. Yet they did these stupid things. Yet, obviously, the word *stupid* cannot be used, not in this context of high holy endeavour.

When the news hit Britain, or England, that these five heroes had died, the nation went into mourning.

"For God's sake look after our people," Scott, dying in his sleeping bag, had written—as well he might, given the record. And the British government, thus publicly put on the spot, did so.

A few months afterwards began the First World War. Now most of us look back and marvel at the sheer stupidity and waste of it all. Not possible that, first of all, it could have been allowed to start; and then, that it was allowed to go on. Impossible that such slaughter could have happened at all. Impossible, impossible—they all must have been mad.

"God be thanked Who has matched us with His hour," sang that young idealist, Rupert Brooke, while millions of young men were being murdered in conditions of criminal negligence.

This note of Brooke's, as of some other poets before the truth of that war came home, was exactly the note of the 1910–13 Scott expedition to the Antarctic. I wonder if the national intoxication over the death of Scott and the others contributed to the mood that made that war possible?

But it could have been no more than that: a small addition which helped to heighten the mood, for all of Europe was drunk with rivalry. So strong was the atmosphere that, for instance, socialists, meeting only a short time before the war began, pledged themselves not to be carried away by the propaganda, not to allow the workers of Europe to hate each other on nationalistic grounds, or to tolerate their being used as cannon fodder for competing empires. For these people were able to see their situation with clarity *before* the drums started beating. But they were not able to stand out against it all; they succumbed and were swept away with everyone else.

It will have been seen by now that the 1910–13 expedition to the Antarctic has for me the quality of extremes meeting, of violent inner conflict, of the high drama that results from such tensions. Sometimes the nature of a historical process, or event, or crisis, is summed up in one person, and I think the person here is not Scott, but Wilson. It seems he was the moral focus of both expeditions. The men came to him for advice, for comfort, for support. They revered and admired him. They respected him and they loved him. They spoke of him in the terms used for leaders and exemplars. Far from it, that he was in any kind of rivalry with Scott: the two men were the closest of friends.

I have to insist that this was an entirely admirable man, whose life was something of a marvel—and to go on insisting, because in the climate or mood we are in now, men like him make us uneasy. It is amazing enough I have to make this point: to my parents, for instance, it would have seemed impossible that such a man could ever have needed defending. But we look at Wilson from this side of two world wars and many "small" wars; revolutions major and minor, and the preparations for the Third World War. We have reason to be suspicious of nobility: noble thoughts can breed murders and murderers. We have learned that truth the hard way.

Edward Wilson was a noble man.

In the first place he was a Christian; a real one, I mean, whose religion underpinned his life, his every thought, from childhood. He came from a line of Quakers, and his parents had no doubt about how this son of theirs should be brought up: they knew what was good and what was bad in those innocent times.

He was perhaps first of all a naturalist: his love and understanding of birds and animals showed in him as a small child. His talents as an artist developed in the service of his studies in biology. He became a fine artist, though he was never trained in any way; the drawings and watercolours he did for the expeditions are not the work of an amateur. He was an outstanding medical student and then doctor, but ill health ended that career. He got tuberculosis, probably because of asking too much of himself. He ate very little, dressed just this side of raggedness, and worked, well, obviously, much too hard.

> *I can't bear people who always take for granted that one's main object is to save up one's health and strength, eyesight and what not, for when one is sixty. How on earth can they tell whether one is going to reach thirty? I think it's better to wear a thing while it's good and new, patching the odd corners as they wear out, instead of putting it away carefully year after year till at last the moths get in, and you find it's no good when at last you think you will wear it.*

He was up every morning in time to do two hours work on his own version of an exegesis of the Gospels: he was not the sort of person to be satisfied with other people's thoughts. He then walked from his modest lodgings across the park to St. George's Hospital, did his stint there, walked back, helped at a boys' club—the boys were as poor as people could be then, bone-bare hungry poor. He worked half the night. He was the kindest of sons, the best of friends; he was . . . but where does one start with such a man? He struck everyone from early childhood as remarkable, and the biographical writings are more like collections of tributes.

> *I knew Wilson intimately, both at Cambridge and at St. George's, and of all the men I have known he stands out by reason of the beauty of his character and the highness of his aims. As an undergraduate he lived a life of ascetic purity, but he was quick to make friends and saw the good in the wildest undergraduate, for his purity was of the quality of flame which need fear no contamination. With even the lighter-minded undergraduates he was immensely popular, for he possessed*

*that certain passport to the College's heart—a vein of delight-
ful humour. No one could meet him without being the better
for it, and it falls to few men's lot to be so deeply loved by his
friends . . .*

A biographer, George Seaver, summed him up:

*Sufficient to say that he held with an unalterable conviction
that there is no situation in human life, however apparently
uncongenial, that cannot be made, if God be in the heart,
into a thing of perfect joy. That in order to attain this ultimate perfection one must live through every experience and
learn to love all persons; that the love particular should lead
up to the love universal; that the worth of life is not to be
measured by its results in achievement or success, but solely
by the motive of heart and effort of will; that the value of
experience depends not so much upon its variety or duration
as upon its intensity; and that by one single whole-hearted
concentrated effort a brief life might attain a level that ages
of ordinary development would fall short of, so that a man
who lives his life thus "having become perfect in a little while
fulfils long years."*

"These are big words," he goes on; and indeed they are. Yet words
of this degree and kind were felt by so many people to be applicable
to Edward Wilson.

Was this man not a saint? Surely he had all the qualities of saints,
in or out of monasteries? What do saints possess in the way of
strengths, love of God, self-tamings, love of their fellows, that
Wilson did not possess?

Nor was this an effortlessly "good" man, for he had to work for
his self-discipline; though it must have helped to have been brought
up in a family where to be honourable and kind and self-controlled,
and the rest, was considered desirable. On the contrary, it was hard
for him. His childhood was afflicted by wicked tempers, perhaps
because too much was being asked of him? He was intolerant and
critical: school-friends feared his "looks of contempt" and his
"scathing tongue." Yet on the expeditions, in conditions where we

all know irrational hatreds and irritations can possess normal friendly people, situations where other people were stressed, morose, difficult, unreasonable, Dr. Wilson remained "cheerful, helpful, balanced, always in possession of himself." He had learned not to condemn nor to criticise. And yet, quite apart from the demands the work of the expeditions made on him, he was engaged in secret efforts of his own—secret because he did not speak of his spiritual life to his colleagues; they did not know the source of the strength everyone felt in him, they had to find out about him later, in his letters and his diaries.

> *Here we have no abiding-place—and I feel it more as I grow older and the days for service and for doing and for making often seem so few ahead and so few behind too. It is amazing and most puzzling when one tries to think what is the object of our short life on earth—a mere visit—and how desperately this must represent our effect on the little part of the world with which we come into contact. I get such a feeling of the absolute necessity to be at something always, and at every hour, day and night, before the end may come or I have done a decent portion of what I was expected to do; each minute is of value, though we so often waste hours and hours, not because we want rest, nor because as sometimes it is a duty, but out of sheer want of application . . . The more one does the more one gets to do . . .*

This man was the stuff fanatics and bigots are made of, in religion and in politics, and he was not one, he certainly was not, and yet . . . perhaps he was, just a little, mad?

There is that Winter Journey, which he insisted on against Scott's advice and went through with, and which so magnificently brought out all his qualities—and from which young Cherry-Garrard never recovered.

And yet he often did not allow himself to go off into extremes, when you would expect it: there was his attitude to *England*, for instance; but he wept at what England did, in the Boer War, and his attitude toward his beloved country was shared by as small a despised minority as the few who, a short time later, hated the Great War. I wonder what Wilson would have made of that war, with its stupidities, its beastliness? And no, it is not easy to decide, and that is what makes the fascination of the man.

> *Everyone is too much afraid or too selfish to be "quixotic" even in little things. Everyone lives by a rule of thumb—by the laws of Society, or the laws of the land, or the laws of the Church, or what not; whereas no one is bound by anything but the law of his own conscience.*

This afternoon I went to a book fair organised by a charity that sends aid to the starving Third World, Oxfam, and there I picked up Admiral Edward Evans's book about the 1910–13 expedition: *South with Scott.* It is breezy and matter-of-fact. He does not say that the ship he had to command, the *Terra Nova,* was a disgrace, and unkind to men and beasts: not at all, he enjoyed the difficulties. He deals with the Winter Journey as an item among others, though he does allow that the ordeals undergone were perhaps untoward. He mentions that Campbell and his party had to hibernate in that ice pit.

Here is a man who has been taught not to criticise superiors.

> *Certainly no living man could have taken Scott's place effectively as leader of our Expedition—there was none other like him. He was the Heart, Brain and Master.*

Well, it was the spirit of the times.

Back from sociological speculation to this little book of mine. I can't say I enjoyed writing it, for the snow and ice and cold seemed to get into me and slow my thoughts and processes.

Or perhaps something else was going on. I finished writing it the day after the death of someone I had known a long time; though it did not occur to me to make connection until then. It took her a long cold time to die, and she was hungry too, for she was refusing to eat and drink, so as to hurry things along. She was ninety-two, and it seemed to her sensible.

It seems to me that we do not know nearly enough about ourselves; that we do not often enough wonder if our lives, or some events and times in our lives, may not be analogues or metaphors or echoes of evolvements and happenings going on in other people?—or animals?—even forests or oceans or rocks?—in this world of ours or, even, in worlds or dimensions elsewhere.

A NOTE ON THE TYPE

The text of this book was set in Electra, a Linotype designed by
W. A. Dwiggins (1880–1956). Although a great deal of Dwiggins'
early work was in advertising and he was the author of the standard
volume *Layout in Advertising*, Mr. Dwiggins later devoted his prolific
talents to book typography and type design and worked with great
distinction in both fields. In addition to his designs for Electra, he
created the Metro, Caledonia, and Eldorado series of typefaces, as
well as a number of experimental cuttings that have never been issued
commercially.

Electra cannot be classified as either modern or old-style. It is not
based on any historical model, nor does it echo a particular period or
style. It avoids the extreme contrast between thick and thin elements
that marks most modern faces and attempts to give a feeling of
fluidity, power, and speed.

This book was composed by The Maryland Linotype Composition
Co., Baltimore, Maryland. It was printed and bound by American
Book–Stratford Press, Saddle Brook, New Jersey.

Typography and binding based on a design by Camilla Filancia.